To

M

Each Day
is a Farewell

Best wishes
+ enjoy the read

Translated by
Anne-Marie Faulkner

Anne-Marie Faulkner

Printed in 2021 by Shanway Press,
15 Crumlin Road, Belfast BT14 6AA

Cover design: Rita Pimenta

ISBN: 978-1-910044-35-3

First published in French by Seuil

Sinon l'enfance, qu'y avait-il alors qu'il n'y a plus?
Saint-John Perse

Apart from childhood, what else have we lost?

Pour vous, ceux de la tribu,
les frères et les soeurs, à qui je dois tant...

For you, those of the tribe,
my brothers and sisters, to whom I owe so much...

Chapter 1

Last night, Yves told me that he had passed by the front of the house, in Trans. He asked me if I knew who lived there now. I haven't the slightest idea who lives there. I don't even know when the house was sold. A short time after the death of my mother, no doubt. I hadn't wanted any part of it. I turned a blind eye to it all. 'Do what you want with it', I said. Sell it, it makes no difference to me, I don't want to know. It doesn't interest me one bit. For all that it's worth, that house. Stuck in between two streets. Wedged between two other houses. And the plot belonging to it? A small yard on the other side of the road. A house which was held up by the wallpaper, that's how bad it was. The rooms divided and then sub-divided to make bedrooms. No heating. One storey? A wretched house. That's what it was. So, sell it on to whoever wants it. What harm can that do me?

Yes, that's right. That's what I told myself at the time. Wasn't it bad enough that Yves spoke to me about it last night, and that I am startled with the idea that other people live there now, live in our house. And that is too much for me. How long did we live there? Well, I was six years old when we moved there and I was twenty-five when my mother died. There you have it: twenty years or so. It's been over twenty years since the death of my mother and yet somehow, I'll never be able to speak about the house in any other way, apart from it being *ours*. So, get out you intruders, you trespassers! Get lost! This house doesn't belong to you. It's ours. We lived through too many experiences, which were too powerful, too intense. We were so happy and sometimes, too, so totally in despair, all of us, all ten children. And our parents.

I live far away from Trans now, and have done so for a long time, away from it all. But sometimes I go back to Brittany, to Trans and pass by the house, absolutely trembling. I just want to quietly peek in through the window, to see what's become of the inside. But it's like I'm burning up, when I approach the window. I can't look, it's simply impossible.

Yves is my oldest friend. We met at boarding school when I was ten and a half. I was going into first year while he was in the year above. Sometimes we lost contact for a year or two, but we always met up again. Eventually he came back to Brittany, while I stayed on in Paris. I pass by the house less and less now, so from time to time I take out old photos. This one for example, of my mother and two of my sisters, in the kitchen in front of the fire. They're laughing. It's evening time, after dinner. I look at the photo and I want to enter it; to go into the kitchen, sit down and listen to them. How could we have been so happy? I know that photos can lie, that we can make them say whatever we want. A husband and wife smile at the lens and we make up, from looking at them, a complete love story, a tale of utter happiness. For all I know, then they were bickering right before the photo was taken. If that's the case, then they hate each other and are going to separate. But, instead they smile for the camera. They lie. Just like the photo lies. But this photo, the one of my mother and my two sisters in the house, in Trans, I know is not lying because I experienced this moment myself and many others like it. It is a happiness which kills me and which I cannot look at for more than a few seconds. So, I shut the album straight away and quickly try to think of something else. Because, although there was so much happiness, there was also so much pain.

Chapter 2

But before I tell you about the house in Trans, I have to first talk about the others. The one in Mortain, where I was born. Trans is in Brittany, with just a few hundred inhabitants, overlooking the bay of Mont-Saint-Michel. Mortain is on the other side, in Normandy. My parents, who came from Brittany, settled there towards the end of the 30s, as my father being a countryman like his parents before him, had found work there as a farm labourer. Paid a pittance and worked like a dog. One day, he finally had enough of being exploited and he became a road maintenance worker. At least then, he could bank on a wage coming in at the end of every month.

The house in Mortain, in Aubrils, to be precise, was a wreck in the middle of a field, at the edge of a forest. One single room for all the family. Ten at the time: my parents and eight children. How did they cope? I haven't the slightest idea. When we left the house in Mortain I was just six months old. I came back later to see it though. A real dump of a place. Today, there's just the field as the house was destroyed. I have one photo, just one, taken from a distance. I look at it and try to imagine what daily life was like, through all that time, year after year. I made my brothers and sisters tell me everything. They fed me scraps of information, snippets if you like.

But, what they really wanted to tell me was something else altogether – the War. The true history of the family in Mortain was the War. The summer of 1944, when everything changed forever and which erased, within familial recollection, years of communal life in the little shack. The landings. The arrival of the first American parachutists, emerging from the forest. The terrible counterattack by the Germans, the SS division of the Das Reich, coming back up from Oradour, pushing the Americans back. The battle of Mortain, taken by some, then retaken by others, finishing in ruins, bodies lying next to bodies. Especially the following calamity: our family outside in the garden, in the middle of eating their meal. Bomber aircraft appear overhead and everyone looks up, eyes to heaven. Suddenly, bombs start going off all over the place and my parents and brothers and sisters hurry towards the ditch behind the house. Just at that moment, a bomb falls in the garden and explodes. My mother is hit by three shards. My father goes to the neighbouring farm for help, barely two hundred metres away. He is obliged to crawl, as machine gun shots follow the bombs. It takes him nearly an hour to go those two hundred metres, before knocking on the neighbour's door, who is convinced that we have all been killed. During all this, under this hail of iron, my sister Agnès, is forgotten about and left in her pram under a tree. A bombshell snaps off a branch in its entirety, right above the pram, but Agnès isn't hurt. The family will forever refer to this as a miracle. A few days later, American soldiers call to our door. To put an end to it all, they are going to destroy everything, brick by brick. They urge us to leave at once and to go as far away as possible. And so my parents leave straight away, their six children in tow, pushing the pram along the roads of Normandy, to try and get to Brittany. Mortain is hell. But it's no different, en route war is everywhere. At the slightest sign of trouble, you have to hide in the ditch, and wait with bated breath. My mother's wound gets infected and she is cared for by an American doctor. They finally reach my aunt's farm in Combourg, Brittany. It's summer, the month of July and it's harvest day at the farm, party time. Here, the war is light years away. My parents and brothers and sisters are not able to say where they've come from, what they are running from nor what they have escaped.

With the war finished, they go back to Mortain. Many of those who had not wished to leave are dead. The town is almost completely razed to the ground. The little shack, is still standing however, in the middle of the field and they move back in. My brother Jacques is born there a year later. And then me, a year after that.

This is the story of Mortain in our family legend. A few nightmarish weeks and a real miracle to have survived it. But over the years and after having listened to successive accounts of it all, what a wonderful western it makes! We, the youngest ones, never got bored hearing about this epic story. Indeed, we were jealous of not having lived through it. It became a real obsession for us, as if everything stemmed from it, which united us, the family. We went back to Mortain years later, to see where it all had taken place, the same areas of forest, and to learn every detail; the battles, the shrapnel, the soldiers. My mother had taken spent shell casings and machine gun bullets which she carefully polished every day and which took centre stage on our sideboard. All throughout my childhood and adolescence, I saw those spent shell casings and machine gun bullets artistically placed on the sideboard, gleaming with a thousand lights. We devoured books, brochures and magazines which recounted the battle of Normandy, to unearth the few pages dedicated to the battle of Mortain. Later on, it became a fascination for war films: we could relive the footage, under a hail of bullets; the family legend. Our life is there, in those few square kilometres, devastated, torn apart, from where we emerged alive. Heroes of a time, which has its very own place in the history books: the Liberation of France! Big words, big sentences, which roared in our childish minds, forever alive in our imagination. What a difference from the other war, the Great War of 1914-1918. All throughout my childhood, I saw women in black, grand-mothers, great-aunts, in perpetual mourning for their husbands killed in the trenches or killed after the war by the filthy gas which poisoned them. A heavy, sinister atmosphere prevailed through framed pictures on sideboards, memories of a catastrophe which annihilated families. Our own war, that of the Americans against the SS, was an incredible reservoir of tales and adventures. My oldest brother told us how he had seen the first Americans emerging from the forest, near the house. It was more enthralling and more thrilling than all the stories we read in magazines. The war, it was us.

At the beginning of the 50s, when we moved to Trans in Brittany, I regularly came back to Mortain, on holiday with my godfather. I remember it as a strange town at that time – I was seven or eight years old – half-destroyed, half-rebuilt. There were loads of wooden shacks, quickly thrown up to house, temporarily, those who had lost everything. Only the 15th century church, la Collégiale, in the heart of the town, had remained intact. A miracle. These are the black and white images, although a little fuzzy, which move and quiver in my mind and memory like ghosts. On the road, on the way out of Mortain, would I again see the little house in the middle of the field; the shack where I had been born. And naturally, during the holidays, I played war games with a friend that I hooked up with every summer. Even today, when I pass through Cotentin in Normandy, I am fascinated by these market towns completely rebuilt by the Americans; all along the same model. And by the cemeteries of white crosses, filled with English, Canadian and American soldiers, all dead in the summer sun of '44. It must be a sickness, this fascination for what happened there, over 50 years ago. But I guess with time it could heal itself. But there you go, that's what it is, our history; Mortain, the war, the Americans and the SS. We were born there, us, the family. All mad because of it, for sure.

Chapter 3

Three years on in 1947, we moved house. It marked the end of the ten of us living in one single room in Mortain. We were, instead, installed in Teilleul which was around ten kilometres away. My father had garnered a new job for himself: from a road maintenance worker, he became a chief road maintenance worker and was appointed to the town of Teilleul. We moved into one of those little wooden shacks which had been designated for us, as we were deemed "war victims." It felt like pure luxury with a total of three rooms! But it is destroyed now, the little shack, just like the one in Mortain. I still have memories from this period however; from nursery school or picking cherries with my brother Jacques en route to school. We made little expeditions onto landfills and refuse pits. Isn't it mad how we loved that? We spent hours scavenging there, trying to retrieve broken toys, old tin boxes, springy gadgets and other odd objects which fed our imagination. It didn't matter what it was, if it appeared useful to us, we took it. We took our findings home to the shack, and our brother Henri, now a mechanic, who loved to build things, would make us something new. These are just some small, trivial memories that have stayed with me.

A shack in the heart of the countryside, two kilometres from the town, at the Saint-Patrice roundabout. The road, straight as a die, which we took to go to school or to mass on Sundays. I have this photo (taken by whom, I wonder?) of the three of us; my sister Agnès, my brother Jacques and me, all in our Sunday best, hair freshly combed, on our way to mass. I must be around five years old. I'm wearing a knitted jumper, made either by my mother or my sister Monique, with two little pompoms. I look a right idiot with those pompoms! Sometimes, I made the journey on the carrier of Agnès' bike. From the town to the shack, it was straight downhill and Agnès, scared stiff, would close her eyes and hurtle on kamikaze style, right around Saint-Patrice roundabout! And yet we never had an accident. Now, if that doesn't constitute a miracle, then what does?

My oldest brother Jean was at boarding school, far from Teilleul and Normandy. When he came home on holiday, we would go and wait for him at the bus stop. The bus was red, with a big spare wheel attached onto the back. As it came by the Flers road, we called it the 'Flers bus.' It seemed to me that Flers was on the other side of the world. I really believe that waiting for and then the arrival of the bus from Flers in the evening was one of the biggest events of my childhood in Teilleul. Since then, I have always loved waiting at train stations, airports, metro stations. It doesn't matter where. Waiting for someone is pure happiness. Jean was coming from somewhere far away, from his school in Maine-et-Loire. It was a fascinating, mysterious world, with its rites and customs. He brought back with him words and expressions and a certain way of being. All this ran light years away from our little existence in the shack in the middle of the countryside. When he got off the 'Flers bus', it was like a giant gust of fresh air, from some kind of mystical world. Another world, of which I only knew snippets. Later, I too would go on to boarding school.

And then in Teilleul, my sister Madeleine and brother Bernard were born and we were finally complete. Our parents and their ten children. We would be labelled a large family for life, with a perfect ratio of boys to girls (five on each side!) which did nothing to prevent and arouse oohs and aahs of admiration and disbelief from everyone and anyone. A large Breton, Catholic family. A picture-perfect image. Already, during the war, my parents had been extended the right to a beautiful diploma of acknowledgement from the French State, signed by Maréchal Pétain, the inventor of the large family moniker. Later on, we would receive the West-France prize, along with our photograph in the paper. And the Nestlé prize, likewise. Each time, there was a grand ceremony with a meal and speech in the presence of the highest civil and religious authorities. However, it certainly wasn't as straightforward as it sounds; you had to demonstrate excellent school results and more importantly an irreproachable moral conduct, which had to be requested from school headmasters. We were ashamed to ask for them, but yet proud to receive them. The press suggested to the masses that a big family had to be beyond reproach. Incidentally there was, into the bargain, a sum of money, reward for all our virtue, which essentially comprised of our contribution to the repopulation of France. The baby-boom. That was us. We weren't ashamed of that money because we really needed it. A big, Breton, Catholic family and without a penny. But here's the bigger picture: a shedload of uncles, aunts, cousins and second cousins, male and female. All country people. Or more originally, on my mother's side, pig sellers.

And fittingly, here's what was announced, after years in Normandy, the great return back towards the family cradle: the region of Dol, Combourg. After Teilleul, my father was designated to Trans, where we rocked up one day in the summer of 1952, to this badly constructed house, all dented, which was practically held up by the wallpaper. And which was to forever be our one and only true kingdom for centuries and centuries. Amen.

Chapter 4

That is my first memory of moving house. From the shack in Mortain to to the shack in Teilleul, from one shack to the next. I have no exact recollection of it of course: I was only six months old. Precocious, perhaps, but all the same.... Moving house is a complete adventure. Waking up at daybreak, followed by a lorry trek through unknown countryside; countryside I had never seen before, through mysterious little roads which went all the way into this Brittany where I had never set foot. Seventy kilometres away at the very most, to the end of the world.

We arrive in Trans by the Pleine-Fougères road (the main town of the district) and come to a stop sign at a big crossroads with the road to Saint-Malo. Just beside the crossroads, near the corner was the house. Our house. There you go, that's it. From the outside, it seems a bit strange. We'll understand why later on, when it will be explained to us that it used to be a café. We go in and find ourselves in a large room. Well, it appears large to us. Not that big though. Not large at all, when everything is considered. At the back there is a storeroom, and miracle of miracles, a staircase. A house with a staircase! We go up, our hearts racing. Upstairs – two bedrooms and a corridor, which leads to a door. Behind this door, to our complete excitement, was another staircase.. This second staircase – dark, disturbing and mysterious – leads to an attic, which is just as dark, disturbing and mysterious. It seems gigantic to us, with little nooks which we can just about make out, beams from which harnesses hang and leather leashes with draught horse collars attached. We grope our way forward a little, almost hitting our heads against beams and whacking ourselves against funny objects and bizarre tools covered in spiders' webs. As for the café, the explanation will come later: in the past it had been the house of a saddler, he who produces the yokes and collars for horses. We understand straight away that this attic which frightens all of us a little and is two whole floors up from the safety of the ground floor, will be our domain, that we will spend days up here playing, dreaming, building, inventing different lives and adventures, getting lost up here conjuring up delightful scares.

For the rest, this house is anything and everything. There is no running water (so no toilet or bathroom), but that's normal for us, as we never had one. The electricity is completely lousy, so Monsieur Marchandet – a friend of my parents from Mortain – makes the trip to fix everything and miracle of miracles, it works. We must cut the storeroom in half to make a bedroom downstairs, which will be the boy's room. The girl's room and our parent's room will be upstairs. Naturally, there is no heating, but again that's normal as we never had any. The only heating will be downstairs in the kitchen. There will be no heating in the bedrooms except in the girl's room, where we will install a little stove.

We then come up with names, to designate the rooms. The big room (big….well…) downstairs will be 'the kitchen' and the store will be 'the room'. Why did we call the store the room? I haven't the foggiest. In any case, it's really practical. If my mother says, 'Get me the butter in the room', I know where it is. It's in the room, easy. There in the store cupboard press, a little hut with a wire mesh where we store the food. It's certainly not as practical as a fridge, but we don't even know that fridges exist. In the room, there are also two barrels of cider, some bikes, shoes and tools. An indescribable amount of junk. And then the dog. That's where he'll sleep, on the mat at the bottom of the stairs.

In the kitchen, nearly all the space is taken up by the table, an immense table: but it does what it has to. There are, after all, twelve of us when Jean is home on holidays from school. Apart from that, there is a sideboard, an incredibly old one, with shell casings on it as well as machine-gun bullets, polished every day by my mother. Chairs, benches, a wood and charcoal stove and a hearth (where my mother makes galettes). So, there you go. Ah, yes: against all the odds my mother will try to maintain a stretch of polished wooden floor, the length of the wall thirty centimetres wide. This strip of polished floor is Mum's pride and joy. We may have been squeezed in on top of each other and it may have been a worn-out and decrepit old house, but that stretch of floor, if that wasn't perfect then nothing was. It was certainly not a great idea to go onto it with muddy shoes or you would be sure to get a good telling off. This patch was Mum's daily victory, her war against everything that we didn't have. It was a signal, a message. 'There is pride', she would often say. She was without doubt very proud. And she wanted us to be proud too.

Inevitably, given the number of children and the lack of furniture, there were several of us to a bed. Head to foot if need be. This bolstered conversation and discussion late into the night, especially in the girl's room. In the winter, we heated ourselves with bricks. We put the bricks into the oven in the kitchen in the evening time. When they were piping hot, we wrapped them up in newspaper. We put them at the bottom of the bed a little before bedtime. The time that it took to heat the bed. When we slipped in between the sheets, our toes would search for the newspaper and oh, what a delight! Naturally, the bricks got cold in the end up. By morning, we were frozen. This was the quintessential way to get chilblains. How we were burdened with chilblains! We heated water in a big basin and took turns soaking our swollen toes in it to soothe them. At least it was something.

Later, as the years wore on, we created other bedrooms. We divided the girl's room in two. We put up a partition in our parent's room, so that Jean could have his own room. Then we split Jean's room in two, so that I could have mine! I was fifteen years old. My first bedroom. Naturally enough, there was just enough room for the bed and just enough space to get into Jean's room (which would later become Bernard's room). There was no window of course. It was a dark room. No matter. I only used it in the evening or at night. Agnès, also had her own dark room next to mine. We used to tap the partition with our fingers to send each other secret messages.

We went in to the town well for water, with one basket in each hand and a barrel hoop for good balance. Or else we took pitchers to

Monsieur Touquet's pump – a builder who allowed us to use it. We washed ourselves in the kitchen with a basin and jug. Our toilet? A hut in the yard. Because there was a yard, on the other side of the road (the one behind, the Pleine-Fougères road). Just one yard. This was a change from the field in Mortain and the garden in Teilleul. It was not even in front of the house. On top of that, there was always the road to cross. But sure, we got there quickly enough.

A wall, by the side of the road, with a little door and that was all. It was pure bliss. The yard was not big by any measure and was extremely cluttered. Apart from the outdoor toilet, there were trees (apple, pear, and a huge hazelnut tree), a chicken coop, rabbit hutches, firewood, clotheslines, and large cut stones, piled up in a corner, on top of each other. We never worked out why they were there. The rest of the yard was for us, the children. Not much perhaps, but enough for us to invent a thousand different worlds and a thousand different adventures, day after day, week after week. We traced a whole system of roads into the ground; all extremely complicated with roundabouts, bends, bridges and tunnels for our little miniature cars. The chickens would come regularly and ruin everything, looking for worms with their claws. We would yell at them and chase them off our circuit and then we would start all over again. And there you have it. Or else, we'd play at shop. Everyone would open their own shop – the grocer, the baker, the butcher, the garage man. It used to take us hours, even days creating the shops of our imagination. Then we would go from one to the other doing the shopping. I remember that there was always 'American cabbage' at the greengrocer's. It was only plantain, but we had re-branded it to make it sound exotic. However, the most exciting thing wasn't doing the shopping but imagining our shops, unearthing from all over all the knickknacks, tools, boards, empty bottles, old tin cans, ads – anything that would make our shop exist and lend it its colour, its personality.

Or else we traced our ideal house into the ground – each one in their own space. And then we would invite each other over to compare and get ideas.

We spent hours of pure happiness there in the yard. My mother, coming in to feed the chickens and rabbits would come over and see what we were playing. We would give her a tour and she in turn would give us ideas.Thanks to her I learned there, how to live with the sun, how to get used to it, to enjoy time, the play of the leaves, the shadows advancing along the ground. When I refer to we, the children, it was of course the youngest – Agnès, Jacques, Madeleine, Bernard, and me. When you're big, you no longer play. One day Agnès stopped playing. And then Jacques. One day, you no longer know how to play. You forget the secret. You no longer understand what it means, or what it consists of. Making up lives and believing in it wholeheartedly. One day, it's all over. It stops suddenly, just like that, from one day to the next. I wonder too if it is not the worst day of your life: the loss of playing, the forgoing of playing games.

We all go through it and one day it was my turn. I made the most of it till the last minute however, indeed to the last second. I wonder if I didn't beat a kind of record: for the child who would play the longest. It was like a gift from Heaven. I remember the day when a friend the same age as me came by to see me in the yard, and caught me playing with Madeleine and Bernard. The tone of contempt in his voice, when he launched at me, 'What, you still play, at your age?' Yes, I still played. And I sympathised with him, sincerely, for no longer knowing how to play. When you go through that barrier and break through the frontier, it's all over and you can never go back. Ever.

But now I have a word to say about the chickens and rabbits. Chickens are stupid. Especially when they come to wipe out, our little circuits patiently and artistically traced in the ground by kicking their claws. But how do you explain that being in the company of chickens is part of being happy? Their little goings-on, their little activities in the grass or on the ground, their pecking with their beaks and their claws, their little guttural noises, their way of half-closing their eyelids, of raising their head to the sun, of shaking their feathers, of spreading themselves out in the dust. It's mad that that relaxes you, that that puts you in good humour. Look at how chickens live in a yard, in the sun, how they potter around quietly in the dust.

It's a way of living in solidarity with the world – and I'm not talking about eggs.

Rabbits have one considerable advantage over chickens: you can caress them and kiss them. They are sweet, warm and silky. The downfall for them, in comparison to chickens is that they are enclosed all their lives in their hutches. But they don't seem to suffer from that so much. They spend their time chewing with an air of reflection, they blink their eyes, they scratch behind their ear with their paw, then they champ down again. We had a bunch of them, fat ones, medium-sized ones, little ones. The main thing was feeding them. Firstly, there was the chore part: you went with the big basket in the evening after school and picked grass from the embankments along the roads. It was a long and painful process. It's mad how long it takes to fill a basket with grass. But if the weather was nice, the smell of the grass and of the embankments in the freshness of the evening was so pleasant, it almost made up for it. The reward was to get to feed the rabbits. You opened the door of the hutches and there they were all pushing away with their muzzles behind the wire mesh. We would throw them fistfuls of grass and they would scurry over and jostle each other to get at it. We would keep an eye out to make sure that the little ones got just as much as the big ones. With great big mouthfuls of grass, they would chew it and stuff their faces. How it ground between their teeth. They would look at us with an air of contentment. We would pet them and stay there for a while watching them eat before closing the hutches.

Naturally, it must be said, we didn't just raise rabbits for the pleasure of watching them eat. We raised them to eat for ourselves. Once they were plump enough, up, into the pot they went! My mother caught them by the ear and, with a blow of the poker behind the head, she took care of them; all very professional. We were sad of course. Incredibly sad even. But that's what it was like. That's what life was like back then. More rabbits were born. And there you have it. Moreover, I'm not sure if you know this, but rabbit tastes really good. After her infraction, my mother carefully cut off the skin, before turning it inside out onto a fork-shaped branch to dry it out which we would sell to the rabbit skin seller, who passed by the town regularly with his cart crying out, "Rabbit skins, rabbit skins! Anybody for rabbit skin?" Rabbit skin wasn't expensive. But one rabbit skin, and then another one, and another one, in the long run.....

Chapter 5

Now, I must slow down. I have gone too quickly. I have to talk to you about Trans. The town where we deposited our furniture and bags for good, in that summer of 1952. Trans, 800 inhabitants, fifteen kilometres from Dol, fifteen kilometres from Combourg, twenty kilometres from Mont-Saint-Michel. How can I describe this earthly paradise? I know that it's a wasteland in the middle of the countryside, a godforsaken place devoid of interest. That you'd go through it without even paying any kind of attention, en route for St Malo. Yes, yes indeed.

But, during all these years, I lived in Trans as though it had been an earthly paradise. And that's the God's honest truth. I swear, on the head of my rabbits. Okay, at the very beginning, we were a little bit lost. I remember my first day at school, in the school yard. I was six years old. A guy came up to me and asked me my name. I wasn't able to answer him. I turned my back and ran off. It was the first time that someone had asked me what I was called. Before, everywhere, people knew my name. There, in one stroke, I understood that I came from elsewhere. That for the boys at school, I was an outsider. At only ten kilometres away you were an outsider. So, for someone all the way from Normandy..... It has to be said also, that we didn't go by unnoticed. A family of twelve who lands in the town of Trans, with its 800 inhabitants, and sets up in the heart of the town, near the crossroads, gets noticed. It has an effect. Who are these people? Where have they come from? Have they got family here? The effect of the masses already. All these new children who are coming out onto the street, going to the girl's school, the boy's school, to Sunday mass. What a palaver! And then Jean was studying somewhere else at boarding school. It was totally bewildering. Especially since he was quickly followed by Marie-Annick, who became a boarder in Avranches. And the others afterwards. What a strange family, where the children didn't stop, like everyone who rocks up to sit their exams! They kept an eye on us. They saw us as unusual, as right idiots. We had friends who came from Normandy (all the way from Normandy!), family who came from Combourg and from elsewhere (a whole 15 kilometres away).

We realised that it truly set tongues wagging. As we came from elsewhere and knowing that it prompted a bit of debate, we added to it a little, when it came to the clan. In it together as always! As for feeling different, not only did it not displease us, but we emphasised it. We emphasised our difference. We played with it. We lugged it around like an exotic perfume. We knew we served as a focal point for grievances for a good part of the town. It gave us character and we liked that.

And then, very quickly, we fell in love with Trans – a town devoid of anything special or distinctive – which I want to make clear right away. Apart from a church that wasn't too ugly, it was quite attractive actually, but while you find shedloads of beautiful churches in Brittany, there's absolutely nothing in Trans. A main street, the high street. The national highway which goes from St Malo to Fougères. Another road, the Pleine-Fougères road, which goes from Normandy all the way to Rennes. A crossroads between the two, right there where we lived. The church square. Two little streets. And there you have it. That's it. You've left Trans, with barely enough time to process that you had entered it in the first place.

Nowadays, when I occasionally take the train, I see small villages and towns away in the distance. I look at the houses. I imagine the people who live there and I start to wonder: how could anyone live in such a place? How they must be so bored and stifle one another! And then it hits me. I remember that I also lived in a hovel, a proper one-horse town. And that not only was I never bored or stifled there, but I spent wonderful, magical years there. Our whole world was centred in Trans. Everything, absolutely everything.

To begin with, we were explorers, the whole lot of us children. First on foot and then on bikes. Later on again, on scooters. In any case, we didn't have a car, we never had one. Dad went to work on a scooter.

When we had to go somewhere, we always asked a neighbour, like the butcher for example who carted us around in his truck, taking us to the cattle mart. So, we began walking round a bit to get to know the place and quickly discovered the most important part: the forest. A few kilometres from town lay the forest of Villecartier. An immense, mature forest of beech trees and in the middle of it all; a pond. We must have walked a gazillion kilometres to get to that forest and then a gazillion kilometres to get back. Not to mention roaming around it every which way! We'd say to our mother: 'We're off to the forest.' And just like that, she'd let us go, the whole little gang of us, setting off for whole afternoons of walks, games, discussions, bathes and dreams. If we were really thirsty on the way there, we'd stop at the Pont-Perrin stream where a cold, but delicious water flowed and which we eagerly scooped up with our hands to drink. We went up the pathway that led to the castle of Villarmois, a pretentious castle from the 18th century where the Count and Countess lived with their children, who addressed each other formally, which gave us a right laugh! We went through the castle park with its strange enormous rock, carved straight down the middle as though for a trench. It was said that it had been used for human sacrifices years ago, at the time of the druids. We'd continue along the pathway, passing near the farm 'Ave Maria'. We'd walk along the first pond, 'Rufien', then arrive into the forest on a dream-like pathway, under beech trees and covered in moss to emerge at another pond at Villecartier where there was a water mill complete with waterwheel. The water mill of the forest would pump away diligently. We'd go further on to the other side of the pond, until we got to the place we called 'the big dip'. We had the place to ourselves including a little sandy cove where we could kick back with our afternoon snack. And behind us? The immense forest. The water, the light, and the sunlight coming through the trees, the smell of the moss, the sweetness of the shade and the mystery we sensed from the depths of the earth, where all was dark beneath the beeches. We were alone, most of the time, for nobody else came to the forest or to the pond – how times have changed: now people can rent pedal boats in

Villecartier. On top of all that, the forest has been completely slaughtered. Apart from our games and conversations there was complete silence all around us. We all learned to swim there in the pond. But the sea wasn't far away. The closest was Cancale a mere 25 kilometres away. But we were not of the sea, we were of the country. The mild smell of the pond, the water lilies, the insects, the beech branches that brushed against us, the sun shining; it was pure paradise.

Sometimes we toured around what we called the Norman camp. We had discovered curious old remains in the middle of the forest: a ditch which marked out old fortifications, with a pile of stones underneath the moss. We did some research and found out that in Trans in 932, the King of Brittany, Alain Barbetorte, had beaten the Norman invader, sending him – once and for all – to the other side of Couesnon. These old remains, for all we know were the Norman camp. We dreamed about it, our heads full of adventure, like the shaped stone in the park which had once belonged to the druids so long ago. It didn't take much to fire up our imagination, needless to say. We read tonnes of books and devoured even more magazines. We lived in a world of hidden treasures, forgotten things, playing detective or mysterious lords, resourceful and proud children, who of course resembled us completely! Without forgetting the war (remember Mortain!), the landing, the SS and the Americans.

However, there was more than just the forest. All round the town in the countryside were loads of strange places; a ruined castle (that of Haute-Villarmois), devoured by ivy, bramble and nettles; farms with curious names, (la petite Abbaye, la grande Abbaye), that we went to see, our hearts pounding, sure we would find remnants of the knights Templar; streams at the base of the thicket, water mills on rivers, abandoned quarries we climbed, rocks we immediately dubbed cliffs, lost villages down dirt tracks….All this interlacing of back roads all around – a real labyrinth. We never bored of roaming around in all directions, like adventurers dreaming about finding the Golden Fleece. We lost ourselves, looked for shortcuts, discovered little hollow pathways in between embankments, a dome of oak trees or perhaps chestnut trees above our heads. It was dark and jungle-like, this primeval forest, through which we walked blindly, without the slightest idea where we would end up. Over the years, we slowly got our bearings, and we designated some special places as secret bases which only we – or at least that's what we thought – knew about; an invisible kingdom. Similarly, in the forest, there was this stream which ran down through the middle of an assortment of rocks, which we christened 'the enchanted valley', just like in our beloved books. Or, on La Boussac road, in the locality of the Val, at the bottom of a forest grove, you had to follow a little pathway, hidden from the road and then push through branches until you reached a secret clearance where we were alone in the whole world.

Trans had become a magical country; a territory which had completely infiltrated our imagination, and filled each of our dreams, that of the group of youngsters who walked along the road. The names of farms and villages, were as enigmatic as cryptic messages: La Croix Ban, Cruande, le Rocher Toc, les Potences, le Pas Cru, Ville Pican, la Croix de Bois, les Places, la Villaze, Lande Chauve.....We gorged ourselves on mystery, invented thousands of stories, head to the wind, hands in our pockets, free as though in a dream. On the horizon, on the road to Pleine-Fougères, stood the Mont-Saint-Michel. When the weather was nice, you could just about distinguish it through the mist from the heat. In inclement weather such as wind, rain or the cold, you saw it emerging above the bay, so distinctly and precisely that you could almost touch it with your hand. The Mont-Saint-Michel was in of itself a kingdom, a bottomless reservoir of dreams, legends, inventions of all kinds. In one of our magazines there was the commendable story of *La Fée des Grèves (The Fairy of the Strand)*, which took place right there, on the Mont-Saint-Michel, in front of our very noses. Both images stayed in our heads; the Mont-Saint-Michel that we saw, the one which trembled in the mist, on the road to Pleine-Fougères and the other one, this mythical place from a piece of fiction, which made our hearts race. We were living at the centre of the world.

Chapter 6

Town life and daily life centred primarily on school. In Trans, like everywhere in Brittany, there were two distinct schools: the state school and the private school. At the time, we called it secular school and independent school. Or still more plainly, amongst us kids: the red-butts and the owls. Everything had been set in stone since the Revolution, as I would learn later. There had been a great battle in the Dol region between the royalists from the Vendée region and the army of the Republic, led by General Hoche. The result? Victory of the Blues over the Whites; the Republicans against the Royalists. The parishes chose their camp. Since then, the colour had stayed more or less the same. In Trans, they were for the Revolution. Trans was left-wing. But the two powers, the church and the town hall, were almost equal. The rector (in Brittany, we don't have parish priests but rectors) had just as much sway as the mayor. The outcome? We had two of everything. Not only school, but shops as well. There was the lay butcher and the Catholic butcher, the lay baker and the Catholic baker, the lay café owner and the Catholic café owner, etc, etc. It was a question of not making a mistake. If you changed your baker, then just as quickly the word spread like wildfire throughout the town that you had switched sides. For sure. Our family was Catholic. Therefore, independent school. Therefore, Catholic shops. To be absolutely clear, we were right-wing. There was a revolution in the town the day we all became left-wing. We continued to go to Catholic shops – after all they knew us so well – while also going to lay shops. Everyone was all over the place. And that's how civilisations come tumbling down....

And so we went to the independent school. However there were two schools: the girls school and the boys school. It was inconceivable that the two would be mixed. The teacher, in the boy's school, was a priest – the parish curate to be precise, very young and full of ideas. Active learning and all that. The whole shebang you might say. The opportunity of a lifetime. The school consisted of one single class. Everyone in together, the little ones with the big ones. The goal was to obtain the School Certificate. The teacher-priest method was two-fold. One: the big ones taught the little ones. Two: everybody worked at their own pace. Each morning he gave us a worksheet which was a kind of roadmap for the day. He gave us leads and pointers and let us get on with it. We got through it quickly enough. As soon as you had finished, you could go on to the next thing or if you were big, help the young ones. You could take a book from the library and read up on the History of France or study geography in beautifully illustrated manuals. There was never any homework, only freedom and autonomy. While all this was going on, he, the teacher-curate, devoted himself to his second job: carpentry. He loved DIY and working with wood. To this end he had installed a studio, right next to the classroom. So he sawed, cut, planed, hammered and glued. We heard the racket of machines and smelt the sawdust while we worked. From time to time, he'd come by and see how things were going, ask us questions, give a helping hand. Then he'd return to his machines. He had made all the desks in the classroom – a system with a linchpin under the swivel seat allowed the desk to adapt to the height of the student as he grew. During wee break, he played all sorts of games with us like soccer, Red Rover and dodgeball. He got us to make planes out of matchsticks. With the aid of an elastic propeller, we wound it up and let it go. The plane took off and flew for about thirty seconds before falling to the ground. We'd stick everything back together and begin all over again. Naturally, he could also be strict. He spanked us with his large hands – like washing paddles. Jesus, it was sore. But the worst part was the humiliation in front of everyone. It was crucial not to cry. Cruel, the curate. But I suppose no-one is perfect.

Apart from that, it was the school of my dreams. One single class, tailored work, an unadulterated desire and love of learning, the smell of the sawdust, the roar of the fire. Those from the countryside – we were from the town – came with lots of frost and snow on their shoes after their trek to school. We wore grey overalls, clogs, (boots for the girls), or ankle boots with wooden soles under which we'd stick on strips of rubber. When I read, *The Lost Estate* by Henri Alain-Fournier, I understood everything in it straight away. It was my school, my village, my stories and legends. It was home.

There was a blacksmith in Trans. Early in the morning, we were woken by the ping of the hammer on the anvil. We would go to see him after school. There were big bellows and a red flame in the forge. The smell of burned hoof when he nailed on a horseshoe – a good old workhorse, quiet, stoic, with his hair in his eyes. We could stay there in the forge for hours on end; it fascinated us so much. The country people waited, rolled their cigarettes, and chatted while we petted the horse. It was a world of red and black which had not changed since that of our grandparent's and mirrored our reading books at school.

There was also a clog maker who gave out refreshments. We watched him carve out pieces of wood, draw out the shape, hollow out the interior, plane and refine it with all kinds of strange tools which enabled him to sculpt the pointed end and etch the minute decorations onto the finished clog which was his signature. He aligned clogs and clodhoppers of all sizes in front of his workshop, glittering patent leather, which smelled new, and which made you want to try all of them on there and then!

The other attraction was the rope maker who made string. We saw him often: he was set up right beside a little plot of land that my mother rented for her vegetable patch. We came to hoe and weed, water the radishes and pick green beans. And we would watch the rope maker make his string, through a complicated and mysterious process, which I never fully understood.

When we needed to get our hair cut, we went to the carpenter. On Saturday nights, he changed job and cut people's hair in his kitchen. We'd sit around the table waiting our turn. He'd get out his electric hair clippers and, taking his time, quietly cut with a cigarette stuck to his lips and the ash tumbling down our necks. He cut men's hair exclusively. The adults drank, smoked, chatted, shared titbits of local gossip, recalled old family stories, of farms and other properties. We children listened intently, completely taken. You certainly didn't need to be in any sort of a hurry! We left the rope maker's house in the pitch black of night, with our heads well fresh. His style was a bowl cut, completely bare well above the ears and at the nape of the neck. When we got back to the house, the others made fun of us. But it was no big deal as they'd have their own turn soon enough!

Early in the morning the road maintenance workers arrived to collect my father. They'd talk about the work that was going on, eat charcuterie and then go on their way, on bike or scooter. Sometimes, the tarring truck stopped by our house. There was a strong, acrid smell; totally asphyxiating. It went right up to your head. It became a familiar smell however, like the burned hooves at the blacksmiths.

The other smell was the scalded hide of the pig. Right beside the house was a butcher, who owned an abattoir. We were always jammed into his yard, watching him kill animals. It impressed us no end, but we got used to it eventually. What he couldn't stand however, was killing lambs. Indeed, he cried when he did it. The rest, the calves, the pigs; it was his job and we loved being scared while watching him do it.

However, the butcher's yard was also the place for the wash pot ritual. My mother boiled the laundry in a great big wash pot under which a fire like no other burned and it was there, in the butcher's yard, that she could do so quietly. It took time, especially the bedclothes.

Afterwards, mum had to go to the outdoor wash place. That's what we called the washhouse. One kilometre on foot and one kilometre back, pushing the cart full of washing. At the wash place – a pool in the middle of the field with a little shelter of corrugated iron – my mother would kneel on a wooden crate filled with straw, and lather, strike the laundry with the beater, lather again, rinse, strike, rinse, wring…It is all very much an idealised image, the old-fashioned washhouse, an old tradition in our beautiful countryside, but it didn't make my mother dream too much. Whether it rained or blew a gale, she had to go to the wash place, push the cart, kneel, lather, scrub, strike and then come all the way back home with the cart. During the holidays, we went with her and spent the afternoon there. For us, it was yet another adventure. In the field next to the wash place we would play, read and chat. It distracted her and helped her pass the time, just like it did for the other washerwomen whom she met sometimes there at the wash place, and with whom she made conversation. On the way home, we took turns pushing the cart. And then we spread out the laundry which smelled of grass, trees and Marseille soap.

While we had no money, we weren't poor. You knew who the poor people were and you knew what it meant. They had nothing and lived miserably. Us? We never lacked for any of the essentials. The only thing was, the more the end of the month approached, the less we could afford to pay. At the grocer's or at the baker's we'd say, "Mum will pay ye' tomorrow." It was a code which everyone understood, much less the businessowners. It basically meant that we couldn't afford to pay and that we had to get credit – just until Dad's paycheck came in. We were a wee bit ashamed, in front of the other customers, to say "Mum'll pay ye' tomorrow." But it didn't matter. Not really.

I can still see my mother in Thierry's – the clothes shop in Pontorson who did special deals for large families – when it came time to clothe us for going back to school after the summer holidays. Naturally enough we recycled to the max. The advantage of being in a large family is that you wear each other's clothes as you grow up. Clearly, when it came to my turn – fourth boy out of five – the clothes were a bit used, faded and patched up. That's not even taking style into consideration – which no-one even talked about back then! And then my sister Alice, after her School Certificate, learnt the craft of dressmaking while Monique knitted like a pro. Between the two of them and along with my mother, they guaranteed the trend. From time to time of course, we had to buy some new things, which reminds me once again of my mother in Pontorson, in Thierry's; lost in thought, her finger on her lips, contemplating the contents of her purse, while looking at the coat which she had to buy me. She talks to the salesperson and tries to get a discount, or to pay in instalments. She wants to know if there isn't another coat, a little less expensive, similar to this one. My mother, in Thierry's, in Pontorson, her finger on her lips, lost in thought.

One day, running water arrived in the town. A whole team of people got out; an engineer, foremen and workmen. For a whole month they besieged Trans digging drains, laying down pipes, making connections and building the water tower. We played soccer with them on the communal pitch. It was like a great breath of fresh air that came from elsewhere, all these young happy people, full of energy, who went from town to town carrying this new marvel: running water. With them, Trans, in one swell swoop, entered a new era. We became modern. We were no longer a godforsaken little place. We saw progress arrive gradually, as the long black pipes came into the heart of the town. And then one day, the sink was put in, along with the tap. We turned it on…. hey presto the water started to run. Everyone took their turn, we all wanted to try! Laugh all you want: it was a miracle, a real miracle. No more need to go to the well or to the pump. This brand-new white sink and this chrome-plated tap with as much water as you wanted. For days, when I went into the kitchen in the morning, I still couldn't believe it. It was only cold water, naturally enough. We still didn't have a shower, nor bathroom, nor indoor toilet and we still washed ourselves in the kitchen. But that didn't matter so much anymore.

The big clean-up for the young ones was Saturday night. Our mother heated the water on the cooker, poured it into the wash boiler and then up, in turn, we jumped in. We were hidden, all the same, behind a screen, in case a neighbour or friends of someone or other would come in, as would often happen on a Saturday night: visits, with conversation around the table, jokes, laughs, digs at those returning from the carpenter's, newly clipped, cups of cider, cups of coffee…. The laughs, especially. Saturday night was party time with all our family and friends. I recall one evening when this guy came in without having knocked at the door. He said 'Hello', sat down at the table and asked for a glass of wine. My mother served him, the guy drank his glass, wiped his moustache, got out his wallet and asked, 'How much do I owe you?' He thought that the house was still a café, like it had been in the past, before our arrival in Trans. He hadn't passed by there in years, but he hadn't noticed anything different. He had come in, he had seen people and had asked for his glass of red. And my mother, who had never seen him before, served him without asking anything. The house in Trans, was just that: open the door and you're home.

But the real party was when the others came home. After his School Certificate at fourteen years old, Henri was taken on as an apprentice at a garage in La Boussac. Six kilometres by bike, morning and evening. After a few years, he became a mechanic in Combourg where he found lodgings. He came home every Saturday night. Marie-Annick and then Agnès who were boarding at Avranches, came home once a fortnight. Jean only came home for the holidays. Later, Jacques in turn became a boarder in Dinan. A homecoming of one or the other, was a real racket! They were all full of stories: of dorms, cruel teachers, nightmarish horseplay. They even spoke a strange language, filled with references to their surroundings and boarding school rituals. We, the young ones, listened to them completely speechless – we were so excited. Our tales of the school yard or the latest gossip in Trans, all seemed so paltry compared to this magical life in town, at boarding school, with its adventures, intrigue, plots, secrets…I knew that it would be my turn soon and I could hardly wait. I mimicked my brothers and sisters by trying to speak like them for I dreamed of being a boarder. But I remember Jacques saying to me, one to one, 'You don't know your living here, in Trans; boarding school, is a complete drag.'

In the meantime, I was an altar boy. That was yet another thing I had long dreamt about. To shine in the chancel of the church, in front of the whole town, with my red cassock and white surplice, work the censor, the sprinkler, know all the gestures off by heart, all the rituals, be part of this great, sacred procession, become a pro of the High Mass….It has to be said, that Mass, the Sunday Mass at 11 o'clock was, from a distance, the most spectacular spectacle in Trans that was played out almost behind closed doors. The girl from the café-bazaar, Marie-Ange Mouton, played the organ and beside her the shoemaker, Amand Boucher, sang in his wonderful tenor voice and the rector's sermon, up there in his pulpit, and all this ceremony of greetings, genuflexions, large signs of the cross, vestments and the smoke from the incense. The children up in front, the women in the back, the men in a side chapel, the Count and Countess and their children in the very front pew – in a special enclosure – the smell of polish and hair gel, Sunday dress, the result of personal grooming and hats, hymns sung out at the tops of lungs as the sun crossed over the stained-glass windows. What a celebration, my God, what a wonderful celebration…The more liberal types – those who didn't practise anymore – waited in the bistro across the way and at the end of Mass joined everyone in the church square to exchange gossip, hear any news from one another and maybe share a joke or two.

We children were fascinated by it so much that one of our favourite games at home was 'playing Mass.' The role of the priest was either Jacques or me. We made vestments out of old curtains. We knew the gestures off by heart and babbled a quasi-Latin. Jacques saved the sermon for himself; he was unbeatable in describing the torments of hell, the devil, his fork, and the fire that would burn us, much better than the priest high up on his pulpit. Agnès played the role of Marie-Ange Mouton, the girl from the café-bazaar on the organ. Madeleine was the choir and Bernard was the altar boy.

One day, finally, it was for real. After a period of trials and repetitions, I was inducted as a choir boy. To eliminate any risks the rector had decided that the setting of my first professional appearance would be the Sunday morning Mass at 8 o'clock. I was a little bit annoyed to be honest. It wasn't as good as the High Mass, with all its pomp and even more importantly, it's big crowd. Well, so what. At last, dressed up in my red cassock and white surplice, I made my entry into the choir, all solemn, hands joined in front of the priest carrying the precious chalice. At the start, everything went perfectly. I had repeated it to the death – I knew everything off by heart. Up until this great moment in the life of an altar boy: the changing of sides of the missal on its great lectern, between the epistle and the Gospel, with a genuflexion – into the bargain – at the bottom of the altar. With a steady hand, I took the missal and the lectern and looking at the congregation, and as proud as Artaban, I descended the steps of the altar. And then, to my horror, I tripped on my surplice, lost balance and before getting up off the floor, sent the enormous missal and lectern flying through the choir, to the front row of the congregation (which, thankfully was the least crowded: could you imagine the shame, at High Mass?). Everyone laughed, except me, now red as my surplice. These crushing beginnings did not however stop me from becoming a model altar boy thereafter. My favourite part: pouring the incense onto the glowing coals and seeing the smoke rise up towards the stained-glass windows. Breathing in the intoxicating incense, before launching myself into skilful movements with the censer, which made cling-cling noises in the great silence of a Sunday.

But there was more than just the censer and Sunday Mass. Sometimes, early in the morning, before going off to school, it was necessary, as the rector used to say, to 'Go and carry the good Lord'. In other words, to bring the last rites to someone dying. So, off we would go on foot, the two of us, in the morning chill, the priest holding the ciborium and the holy oil and I, following, brandishing a lighted lamp which alerted people that we were going to bring the good Lord. People stopped as they saw us coming and made the sign of the cross. Sometimes we walked a long time, up through muddy pathways to lost farms where the family would welcome us and show us into the room where the dying person was. It was cold, sad and dirty; with the dying person all haggard looking at us with mad eyes. I was afraid and cold. I wanted to go outside and run around in the fields. I wanted to cry out: let me go, I am only eight years old and I don't want to die!

And then it was my turn to become a boarder. I did the exam in Saint-Malo to obtain a grant. I was ten and a half years old. And in the October, I joined Jacques in Dinan, all excited. My big adventure! But it was

Jacques who had been right all along: right from the first night, in this big dormitory, in these sad beds with their cold metal, I was at a low ebb. Why wasn't I at home in Trans, in the kitchen, reading quietly in the warmth with my family? What was I doing in this sinister environment where I knew no-one – apart from Jacques – with this prefect in the next room, keeping an eye on us, and who would wake us up by clapping his hands early in the morning. Please God, make this a dream, or a nightmare, so that I wake up at home in Trans so that I can go out and play in the yard so that I can see the hens and the rabbits, so that I can go get milk at the farm with Bernard and Madeleine so that we can go for a walk in the forest, to the pond at Villecartier... But God turns a blind eye, God has better things to do. I woke up in the dorm every morning. I had wanted to go to boarding school, like the big ones. And now I was there.

And it wasn't one of those boarding schools for non-professionals, who went back home every Saturday night. We only got home for the holidays. Months went by without seeing Trans, our house, family! On the plus side, when we finally did get home, it was party time. We had waited for it for so long and dreamed of the moment so much. But we still had to make our way there.

Jacques and I would take the train as far as Dol. After that, we had to make our own way. Fifteen kilometres: from Dol to Trans – with our suitcases. So, we thumbed. It worked out alright, most of the time. But sometimes, we waited for hours on the way out of Dol or in La Boussac, where we hopped up and down with rage: all this precious time lost, when we had so many things to do in Trans, and so few days ahead of us. Hardly had we arrived home than we would find the others. We would hurry outside, onto our little lost roads, our secret places and our mysterious villages. We would read and catch up on our magazines. We would go to the forest and to the pond at Villecartier. And then the countdown would start, and we would have to take the train back again. Henri, who had passed his driving test, would take us to the train station in Dol in his little Citroen 2CV. The train for Dinan: 17:51, platform B, track 2. The return to the dorm. All my life, I have kept that logged in my head. I'll never forget it: 17:51, platform B, track 2. The return to the dorm and the return to misery.

.

Chapter 7

B   ut what was this misery, compared to this thing which was eating
    away at me, day after day, night after night and which I need to
    address now? Everything has a price. The happiness in Trans,
this happiness that I supped until the very last drop was a lie. There was,
at the epicentre of this happiness, a much greater unhappiness. And I
don't know if I will find the words to go on, to recount this hell on earth.
One day shortly after our move to Trans I understood two things: my
father and my mother no longer loved one another and my father drank.
It was the demise of love and the work of death.

I am going to go slowly here, as I am treading along the abyss. I
found these few lines among my papers which I wrote a long time ago.
I don't remember when I first tried to tell this story but up until now, I
have not managed to do so. It has all been in vain.

Here's what I wrote: 'Well it was evening time and we knew that he
was coming back. Silence round the table. A nervous laugh. The noise
of his scooter. And the storm in my head. He was drunk. Or else
pretended to be. Barged into his chair, sat down, demanded his soup.
And everything started again.'

Everything: the horror of every day. I don't know what happened
between my parents and I will never know. I am not able to explain it.
And I don't want to. I didn't want to know who was in the wrong or who
was in the right. Did my father drink because there was no more love
between them? Or did the love die out because he drank? A child cannot
ask themselves those questions. What I saw and what I was living, was
this wall of hatred between the two of them, this abyss where we were
headed and where we were all going to lose ourselves. Every evening
when my father came home, the war resumed: the cries, the insults,
sometimes even blows between them, the terror which froze us, the
descent to the bottom of a dark nightmare. What could we say, what
could we do, us children? This hatred, this despair with which my

parents lived, how do you fight against that? How do you make it go away, so that things go back to the way they were? Who had the key to paradise lost? Who had the magic wand? At night, every night, in the privacy of my own bed, either at home or at boarding school, I would repeat almost like an incantation my prayer in which I wanted so much to believe;

'Please God, let my parents get on.' In the dark emptiness, this silly talk to which I clung to get courage. But nothing ever happened. Always the war and always the hatred.

So, in order to survive and to protect ourselves, we closed ranks into our own happiness; a child's happiness; our rites, our games, our little enchanted world. It was a bubble of happiness so that we could forget and let on that everything was grand. That's what I tell myself today anyhow. To try and understand how it played out in our heads. How our childhood could be cut in two like this, how it was divorced from itself. A frenzy of happiness – to taste every minute of every day – and the world which falls apart every evening. To live intensely, all together, in the warmth of the clan, when everything is cinders, even in the heart of the family. How long can that last? And at what price for each of us?

The day of my Holy Communion was a beautiful sunny day. I was ten and a half years old and about to go off to boarding school when I came awfully close to the abyss. We had a celebration with the entire family; my uncles and aunts had come from all over – my godfather had come all the way from Mortain, as well as my sister Alice's fiancé. It was the last celebration in Trans before my departure to boarding school in September. The High Mass, the presents, the meal, the laughs, the jokes. All that goes on within a family; the plots, old stories, memories of Mortain and Teilleul… I was bursting with happiness, it was like a farewell to my childhood in Trans, but devoid of any melancholy: a transition, another chapter, surrounded by the warmth of everyone. And then, in the evening time, my father, drunk, got embroiled in an argument with an uncle. There were cries and violent gestures. It was a brouhaha with chairs knocked over. The celebration ended abruptly. My aunts and uncles took their leave quietly, whilst my brothers and sisters were rendered speechless. It was so sudden like someone's death or burial. I was hugged and consoled, but it didn't help one bit. Never had I felt such despair or been so frozen on the inside. I wasn't angry with anyone; I didn't know who to blame. I only knew that something had come to an end. And my magic words that night, in my bed, and all the nights that followed, was that it will never be anything other than more despair.

Chapter 8

My father was a stranger to me. I would have liked to have loved him, but how was that possible when we didn't even know each other? I used to see him leave in the morning with the road maintenance guys, for the worksite of the day. Over the years, he came back from work later and later. Sometimes very late, when we had already gone to bed. To avoid re-igniting the war, no doubt.

I don't think I ever had a single chat with him as a youngster or a single discussion with him as an adolescent. In any case, I can't remember one. I have this image – precious among others – of a game one evening, round the kitchen table. I must have been around seven or eight years old. I was running round the table and my father was trying to catch me. He was sitting in his chair smiling and I was running and laughing like crazy, like someone who didn't quite believe their luck: never had I ever played like that with my father. I would have liked it to have gone on forever, and to begin all over again the following day and the day after that. And then, in one fell swoop, the spell broke: the war between my parents erupted again with cries and insults. The games came to an end, like a wire cut dead never to be up again. It was too good to last.

I have two other memories of my father. The first was when he came to Dinan to visit us one day, Jacques and me. Normally it was my mother who came. Ah, these visits to the poor aul' boarders, all down in the dumps in their dorms! My mother only came a few times a year. She made the journey with the butcher from Trans, our neighbour, who would come to buy cattle at the mart on Thursdays in Dinan. The visits were only for a few hours, so not much time really, but we dreamed about it in the days leading up to it and then thought about it for days afterwards. It was both intense and cruel: we knew it wouldn't last long and that we would once more feel even more down in the dumps that evening; thinking about Trans, our home, and our family. Everything that we missed. It was like a subtle reminder of the silent despair of the first days back at school after the summer holidays: your parents would accompany you, carry your suitcase into the dorm, do a tour of the school, force themselves to laugh and joke. And then they would leave whilst you stayed with the others, these orphans during those first days back at school. It was the end of the summer holidays with the whole year of the dorm ahead of us: autumn, winter, the cold, along with waking up in the middle of the night. So, we pushed ourselves to pretend like everything was fine. We kicked the ball in the school yard, in a near rage, whilst waiting for the bell to go for the first meal in the dining hall, when at the same time in Trans, there was soup on the table under the hanging light...

So, back to my father's visit then; one day he came by on his scooter. I must have been twelve years old. Jacques and I walked with him in the streets of Dinan. Besides any familial walks that my father joined in with in Trans, it was the first time that I walked with my father. He smiled, he seemed happy with his lot. He took us to a pub and had a glass of cider, I think. He knew the owner and they joked together. I can't recall what we talked about, classes and teachers, I imagine, subjects that we preferred, that type of thing. Nothing too personal for sure. Not on our part nor on his. One single and unique occasion to get to know each other. And there you have it: nothing. Just two hours perhaps of walking in the streets of Dinan and then drinking in a pub. And that's it, over. For life. Except that, it was already something to be alone with him, for Jacques and me. It was like a strange dream, to walk around with this man who smiled and who was our father, but of whom we knew nothing intimate or personal.

Why are things like that? Why does your father remain, right to the end, a stranger? Who is he, this man who leaves every morning to go to work and who comes back late in the evening only to re-start the war again? I never went on holidays with him. I never went on holidays with my parents. I never saw them go on holiday or go away somewhere. I knew nothing about family holidays anywhere other than in Trans.

Where would we have gone? How would we have been able to pay? It was something I read about in books: setting off by car or by train to find yourself together in a hotel or some rented accommodation by the sea or in the mountains. It was only in books and definitely not for us.

My other memory of my father was later, maybe one or two years later, when I went to see him in hospital in Saint-Malo with Jacques. He was being treated for a nasty wound on his foot which had reared its head again. A long time ago, in Meillac, on the family farm, a horse had trod on his foot. It was this old wound which had suddenly become infected. And then, that day in the hospital, I saw something extraordinary which has never left me.

The ward was full of other male patients about the same age as my father. He introduced them to us and he proceeded to joke and laugh with them. I saw that he made them laugh, was extremely popular and that they really liked him. I kept that almost a secret to myself: my father was funny; he had a good sense of humour and people really liked him. I had already heard some little scraps of conversations among some of Dad's workmates about how much pleasure they had working with him. Or by those in the festival community that my father had created. Here, I was seeing and hearing him being funny. I was discovering someone else who had been, up until now, completely unknown to me. But it was he who had created the war at home in Trans; the cries and the shouts. Here, in this hospital ward, it was he who was making people laugh. It was he with whom everyone joked. Suddenly, I was seeing everything that I had missed. I had not known this man, this father. I could laugh with him and discover the world with him. But no. It didn't work out like that. And then it was too late. The game was up. In Trans, whenever I came back on holiday, it had gone from bad to worse. We were captives in a story which we couldn't control. It was impossible for us to go back in time, to start again, to try a new path, to alter this course, which was dragging and crushing us. I would never know my father.

What I did know of him in the end, was a place, a house: Chantepie, in Meillac, near Combourg. His parent's house and his childhood home, which we visited regularly. A one room house, with two big beds, a table and a fireplace. There was an outhouse next to it, a sort of granary, where you could sleep. We frequently went there because our grandmother lived there, my father's mother and our only grandparent still alive. She was an adorable little old lady, all stunted, amusing, and full of energy. I didn't know either of my grandfathers because of the war of 1914 and of what had come afterwards. Nor had I known my mother's mother. 'They don't make old bones in our family', I would say to myself. Along with my paternal grandmother lived Rosalie, my father's sister. His brother Jean, a priest, also came by frequently.

His other sister, Anne-Marie, had moved in nearby after her marriage, a few kilometres away in Combourg, on a farm on the outskirts of a castle's park. Yes, that of Châteaubriand. We often went to her house during the holidays where we slept in the outhouse on top of the hay. We minded the cows and the pigs. To tell you the truth, 'minded', is perhaps a bit of an exaggeration. I minded the cows with one eye, whilst doing something else with the other. Reading, dreaming and completely forgetting that I was supposed to be minding the cows, who understood very quickly that they were, to all intents and purposes, being minded and who escaped quietly and peacefully from the field. By the time I noticed, they had gone back to the byre. At the very beginning of the afternoon, that does not go unnoticed on a farm, which let's just say, meant that I quickly developed something of a reputation. With the pigs, it was even worse, I was terrified of them. Big fat gigantic sows, evil and sadistic, who tried to bite my calves. To get away from them, there was only one solution: climb a tree. I looked smarter up in the tree, supposedly looking after the pigs who were taking the mick out of me. Otherwise, there was the harvest and more especially, the big spreads of food which went on for hours with the local farmers, who would come to give us a helping hand.

On the other side of the yard was the castle's park. I had read the wildest passages of *Memoirs from Beyond the Grave*. The young Châteaubriand trembling with fear in the castle tower, the ghost story, and the wooden leg. I felt like I was almost part of the family from seeing the castle, from the bottom of the park. Moreover, he had studied in Dinan, like me, at Cordeliers, like me. I had read this rather melancholic sentence from his quill, where he said that his forced uprooting from the places of his childhood, the woods of Combourg: 'All my days are farewells.' Why do you have to say farewell to your childhood, to everything that you love? Why do things come undone? Why does everything vanish?

My grandmother, my uncle and aunts: that was my father's family. It was cosy, like this old house full of memories, stories and accounts which interwove the family legend. We spoke *patois* – another language – full of little turns of phrase, with old words which enchanted us and made us laugh (today it's called *Gallo* and is taught at university, perfectly). It was warm, but also incredibly loud and heavy, and quite stifling for us children, precisely because of all these memories and all these family stories. We rehashed and repeated the same old stories and the same memories over and over. There were old photos in frames, on the sideboard and you had to know who everyone was, for the hundredth, the thousandth time. This family, my father's family, gave me the impression that they were only interested in the past, in stories of the past. In this little house, which I loved however, with its wild garden, its hens, its rabbits, I had the feeling that I was going to suffocate under the weight of the past. I would say to myself that later on when I was big, that I would never annoy anyone with family stories, of my aunts and uncles, grandmothers and grandfathers, or cousins. The outcome was that I stopped listening to what was being told and that I now know almost nothing about my family's history, on my father's side. All these old stories blocked my memory, so I cleared them out. Today I'm angry with myself. Perhaps I would know more about my father. Perhaps I would have known how to talk to him or how to listen to him. Too late now.

And then, in the year of my fifteenth birthday, my father fell ill. The doctor from Pleine-Fougères came to examine him at the house. I don't know what he said to him or what he said to my mother as I was in Dinan, at school. I just knew that my father could no longer get up and that he had to stay in bed. During the next school holiday, I saw him in bed, downstairs in the 'boy's room'. I found that he had the look of an old man. He was the age I am today, fifty-three years old. He smiled at me and told me that everything was fine, that he would soon be back on his feet again. But we saw the doctor from Pleine-Fougères more and more frequently, who had a growing look of concern. This father who had become, for us brothers and sisters, more and more unfamiliar, who would ignite the war, in the evening, and here you now have us wanting to tell him that we loved him.

I remember I had gone to a youth camp with Jacques and Bernard in the Pyrenees that summer. Just before coming home, at the moment when we were buying souvenirs, we discussed our father's present. I think it was the first time that we ever bought him a present. We chose a lovely knife; solid and rustic. We told ourselves that he would like it, that he would love to have it in his pocket. In fact, we had especially wanted to think that he would use it, this knife. That he would use it for years and years. And therefore, that he would live. Buying this knife was our way of telling us and telling him that we loved him and that we didn't want him to die. We didn't say it to him openly, but gauchely, awkwardly, like three brothers who had never wished to speak about the catastrophe of love and the death of love, in the heart of the family, between our parents. Brothers who had kept silent, who had suffered in silence, each on their own, who didn't dare speak of this father who was pulling away and from whom they were pulling in turn. Upon our return to Trans, we gave him the knife, as a sign that everything was going to start over again, that everything was going to change, for him and for us. He smiled, taking the knife, but his smile said that it was too late.

A little while afterwards, one Sunday, the day of his birthday, he asked for the last rites. I recalled the time when, as an altar boy, I would accompany the rector in the cold dawn down lost roads, going 'to carry the dear Lord' to farms already visited by death. This time round, it was

41

our turn. But I didn't want to believe it. I said to myself that there was nothing to worry about. My father wanted to see the priest and to take Communion, that's all. It meant nothing more, Jacques said. Why speak of the last rites, of the 'sacrament of the dead?' I listened to him and thought the same. After the priest left, my father, propped up against pillows, asked us children to come into his room, to group around his bed. He said a few words of farewell to each of us. Today it is I who write 'words of farewell', because later on, that's how I understood it. But, at this point in time, as it was his birthday, my father simply wanted to unite us all round him and say to each and every one of us how he saw us and what he loved about us. Never had he spoken to us in that way. Never had he told us what he thought of us. Never had he used such words. We were there, round his bed, on this summer Sunday, unsettled, uneasy and completely bowled over. We didn't overdo displays of affection in our family. We played together, talked and laughed and we loved getting together during holidays.

There was a tribal bond between us; this happiness in sharing the same rituals, the same coded messages, the same mythology. But, because of this hurt within the heart of the family, this war between my parents, we didn't know neither words nor gestures of affection or love. And it is he, my father, who finds them. It is he who breaks this silent pact to tell us simply what he had in his heart and what he wanted to say to each of us for so long. Never in a million years did I think I would experience this scene one day. I had read stories of this kind of thing in books and magazines; the father who, at the hour of his death, reunites his children round him. It was out of a novel, fiction. It could never happen for real. And here now is my father with his tired smile, undoubtedly trying to make us forget the distant father, the stranger that he had been, who finds the courage to tell us how much he loves us, much better than any book. It was we who did not know how to respond to him. We are too speechless, too overwhelmed. I was angry with my father for all that he hadn't given us, for this violence in the house, for everything that he had broken in me. But I forgave him for everything, as he was able to find these words, on this summer Sunday. I forgave him for everything.

Some days later, when we are all together in the kitchen (minus Henri, who was completing his military service in Dakar), Monique, who was coming out of my father's room calls to us:

'Come quickly, he's dying.'

We hurry into his room and gather round the bed. My father's eyes are closed, his cheeks hollow. He breaths deeply with more and more difficulty. He opens his mouth and this terrible noise streams out - a noise which is called a death rattle. Someone goes to fetch a priest. It is the rector who comes, my old teacher. He asks my father if he is conscious, if he can hear him. My father nods that he can. The rector recites the prayers. My father subsides more and more, and the gasps become more frequent. There we are, standing silently around the bed. My mother stays opposite my father at the bottom of the bed, her hands placed on the wooden frame. She looks at him intensely, without moving or saying a word. I watch my mother and I try to imagine what it is she's thinking, which images and memories are going through her head. Yes, I look at her and I try to imagine. She must remember, I imagine, their first meeting, their love, their marriage, all these years when they were so happy together. And then the children, and then the war in Mortain – those hellish days when they thought they were going to perish – their miraculous salvation, the return to Mortain and then the move to Teilleul, then their arrival in Trans – and the start of a hellish time for both of them. Yes, I look at her, my mother and it's as though I am reading her thoughts, whilst her husband, my father is in the throes of agony, of death. What happened? Why was there this descent into hell all of a sudden? Could things have been different? They cursed each other for years, and here she is now standing, her arms placed on the wooden bed frame, watching him die. This man whom she so loved, but whom she also so hated.

But the death is a long one. The gasps become ghastlier. I almost want to block my ears. I am frozen with horror. My mother, then, looks at us, the youngest of us, and asks us to go up to bed. I feel a slight sense of relief as soon as I go up to the black hole that is my bedroom. Early in the morning, I go downstairs. 'He's dead', my mother tells me. I go into the bedroom to see him. He has one eye slightly open, which frightens me. He is of a thinness which I could never have imagined. He looks as though he is eighty years old, but it's my father, dead at fifty-three.

I'm fifteen and my father is dead. I walk alone outside on the road to Pleine-Fougères, and I try to understand what is happening in my head. I should be submerged in sadness, I should be crying out all of my suffering and my despair. My father is dead. You are an orphan. I might well repeat these words, but I don't feel myself. I don't know what is happening. I don't know who I am presently or else I am discovering someone in me who frightens me, who shames me: I know that it will no longer be hellish at home, in the evening. That there will be no more fights, no more violence. And, selfish fiend that I am, I breath deeply. I know I shouldn't write these words. But why should I lie to myself? At the same time, I have this image of my father in his bed, his smile and his words of love for each of us. I think back to that walk round the streets of Dinan, with Jacques. To that hospital visit in Saint-Malo. I cry for the loss of the father I could have had. I curse the entire universe for this injustice; my father has died at the very moment when I could have really loved him as a son. Everything has come too late. And now I am going to live with this wound. Worse: I'm going to try and let on that it doesn't exist. Pretend and keep silent.

We take turns in the bedroom to wake my father – for you can't leave a body alone. When it's my turn, I look at his body, his face, these white hands on the white sheet. It is my first encounter with death. I force myself to stay, even though I feel such a fear surge within me, such anxiety. And then, from the second day, there is the smell of the body. Ah, to be fifteen and smell the odour of your father's body. I wanted to open the door, go out into the street and run like a madman. But when your father dies, you don't run in the street. You walk with your eyes cast downwards. You play the role that the people of the town expect you to, the role of an orphan.

The day of the funeral, the church is cramped full. People have come from all over, from the town, the countryside, other villages. My father was well known. My father was loved. Probably more than he was at home, in his own house. At the cemetery, standing in front of the freshly dug out grave, I think back suddenly to our games as children, just after our arrival in Trans. We used to go into the cemetery to look for children's graves, to steal the cherubs laid onto the grey stone. Little painted miniature cherubs, which we found so adorable and who joined our collection of treasure; old toys all patched up, bottle caps, jam jars with pretty labels, little cars, plastic dolls. The cemetery is a playground. The most surprising playground and the most picturesque playground. But here I am in front of my father's grave. I have forgotten the secret of playing. I have lost my childhood. Each day is a farewell.

Chapter 9

My father is dead and there is no money in the house. Gone are the Christmas presents, or that's what my mother tells us anyhow. To get through it, my mother must find herself a job. She has raised 10 children in materially-deprived circumstances, and yet she doesn't stop expending herself; boiling the bedclothes in the washing machine, pushing her wheelbarrow towards the washing place, beating the sheets in cold water, weeding, digging the vegetable garden, feeding the farm animals, preparing the meals, sewing, darning clothes, knitting, doing the housework, shining the bullets and casings on the sideboard, polishing the strip of parquet floor alongside the wall of the kitchen – her pride and joy. Today, on top of all that, we must bring money home to her. Naturally, we boarders are all grant recipients, but even that doesn't go far. The older ones, Alice, Monique, Jean, Marie-Annick and Henri are beginning to work. But that also is not enough to get by. And so, my mother rents her services as a cleaning lady. A maid basically, in the village among the shopkeepers. She plucks game at the restaurant. She is employed at the castle by the Count and Countess. Her so proud and teaching us pride in turn. During the holidays, I sometimes go to see her at the castle, which is not easy for me. My mother there with brush in hand, doing the housework for the Countess and looking after her children. After all her hard work looking after us. In the evening, she cycles home and becomes our mother once more, along with the same household chores to do.

She never speaks about my father. Never talks about him. Complete silence. When I'm at school, I imagine her on winter evenings, alone in that cold, empty house. Alone with her memories. And this willpower to be happy, no matter the cost and in spite of everything she has suffered throughout her life. Her father died very young. Then her mother remarried. She has two half-brothers and one half-sister. Not long afterwards her stepfather died followed by her mother. And then in the summer of '44, the traumatic events at Mortain; the three explosions. And then the war with my father. And then the death of my father. But always, everywhere, this will to be happy. This love for life. How to make the most of every moment of respite. Like for instance, in Trans, putting the chair out onto the footpath on a sunny day, to get some air and talk with the neighbours who have taken out their chairs onto the footpath opposite. Whilst we, immersed in our books and magazines, take advantage of this moment of grace, this blessed time, the soft chat of my mother with the neighbours on a summer's evening. My mother always spoke to everyone; business owners, neighbours, passers-by, friends. She likes the sun, flowers, reading, writing. Receiving a letter from Mum in Dinan at boarding school is a moment of pure happiness. She talks about Trans, the goings on in the village, news of the family, the weather. She is gay, funny – she wants to love life.

And now she is alone in Trans (Bernard and Madeleine are now at boarding school), and I hope that she has enough strength and courage to get by. We bought a television for her. I don't remember when exactly. Years after my father's death for sure. Before that, we used to go watch television at a neighbour's house, Madam Médard, who lived alone. The television was in the kitchen and we pulled our chairs up, squeezing in against each other. We watched soaps such as *Belphegor* or films like *Les Grandes Espérances* which scared the living daylights out of us. Needless to say, we returned home very quickly, in the pitch black, sometimes meeting ghosts along the way. Otherwise, during the summer, we went to watch the mountain stages of the Tour de France, along with music from the Eurovision, tata ta ta ta…..And all the while we went without a telephone. Instead, we went to the butchers next door, picked up the phone, dialled the operator and simply asked for the number. When people called us, it was the same thing: people asked for Trans 9 and the butcher came over and taped on our door. How that must have annoyed him, to have to come and knock on our door! To act as our personal operator! Real progress was made however, with the installation of a shower – complete with hot water – and indoor toilets.

We had to put up another partition in the 'room' on the other side of 'the boy's room.' Finally, there was no more need to cross the road or to hurry through the yard to sit down in the wooden cabin located next to the henhouse.

When we go back to Trans for holidays, it's always great fun. We have a million things to talk about and a million things to do. We keep up our endless walks along the little routes in the countryside and spend entire afternoons in the forest of Villecartier beside the pond. We go back to the magical places of our childhood; these valleys, these clearings, these rocks which we baptised of our own accord a long time ago. But this is already becoming nostalgic. Childhood is over with. The happiness from playing games as well. We gather to talk about those years. We never stop saying, 'Do you remember the time….?'

We have hundreds of stories to talk about, stories of times gone by. You never forget your childhood. You never forget heaven on earth. You want it to go on forever. You want to live in this bubble, feel safe in it's warmth, which would allow you to forget all the other stuff, such as the hell in the house in the evening. And then the death of my father. And this silence amongst us. This huge block of black silence which keeps us from breathing.

The Christmas holidays are, of course, the most nostalgic. This period of grace is woven with rituals like so many threads which go all the way back to childhood and that you don't dare break, so as to let the dream continue. The manger built every year from stones and moss found in the forest. A whole afternoon spent in the cold, collecting holly only to get caught out by the oncoming night. The tranquillity of the house when it is cold outside, the whining of the cooker and a song playing on the record player. And the school dorm light years away. Midnight Mass as well of course. Long ago, when we were young, Mass was preceded by a play performed by the youngsters of Trans, under the direction of the school curate. In the school building a stage was put up in a room next to the classroom. There were magnificent depictions of scenery painted on huge canvases. We brought the chairs from the church to allow everyone to sit down. We acted out some abominable melodramas which elicited every tear we had in us. After the performance, we all took a chair back to the church. And then on with midnight Mass. We continued the habit of drinking a big bowl of hot chocolate with biscuits. And then the discovery of presents: one or two books selected and bought for each of us by our mother.

Chapter 10

But you grow up, you grow older, and you discover the world. The older ones work: Alice already has children and for us, the youngest in the family, our world was gradually changing too. We were making friends, each one of us, at boarding school or elsewhere. Our first trips away, work appointments for a brother or a sister, the mind evolves and the conscience awakens. Politics was breaking onto the scene, other cultures were opening up, such as the Third World, to 'hunger in the world', as we used to call it then. Suddenly, Trans, was becoming tiny. The horizon beckoned. It's all happening. The family bit by bit leans to the left. My father was right-wing with his beliefs and commitments. A large Catholic family, so right-wing: that's how it was. And then it shifts, alters, deviates. The war in Algeria occurs round then. Those years were the time, when you became reflective and serious, when you discovered ideas and rejected injustice and the middle classes.

In Trans, we didn't know what middle class was. We were all the same. Or almost. In Dinan, over the years, I began to realise where I was from and what social class meant. Those who were better dressed, those who had money in their pocket, and whose parents had more noble professions. Me? With my clothes all sewn back together and patched up. My short trousers (or trousers) inherited from my older brothers? I used to say to myself that I looked like a clown. Little slights at boarding school. But, deep down, I didn't give a damn. Unwittingly and without even noticing it, I had found the perfect ceremony: the Awards of Excellence. I had discovered that I was good in class. It is a strange experience to be given top marks and Awards of Excellence in front of others, when that was the last thing you were expecting. It appears I'm taken with cinema – I swear that's the truth. How could a young guy like me from Trans, the son of a road maintenance worker, have ever imagined contending with the people of the town? And there you have it. My revenge: the days of the distribution of prizes in the main courtyard at school, listening to a bigwig, surrounded by all the authorities from the town and around, announcing, 'Award of Excellence, Alain Rémond, from Trans.' What pleased me especially was the 'from Trans' part. It was revenge for all the one-horse towns, for forgotten places, and the forgotten countryside. But the real reward was seeing my mother having come purposefully from Trans, seated in the middle of all these well-dressed people, who heard my name and who watched me come down from the stage with my prize. The look and the smile on my mother's face that day, in the main courtyard of the Cordeliers school, in Dinan. I will never forget it. We are nothing, we have nothing, but an Award for Excellence, due to a love of learning and studying. Against knowledge, money counts for nothing: that is what I read in my mother's look. I know it's a story that has been told many times, an old chestnut that has been read a hundred times for the enlightenment of the masses. I couldn't care less: it's my story, that's all.

At the beginning of the sixties, apart from the war in Algeria, the big rage was the sweeping teenyboppers. The stars here included Johnny, Sylvie, Françoise Hardy, Richard Anthony.... Let me just say it straight away: my brothers, sisters and I were not fans. Not one bit. It seemed cheesy, simple, retarded. But especially (and we're not very proud of the concept): fundamentally alienating. Behind this rage, a method by traders to make the youth forget about the real issues is uncovered. To prevent their waking up to real problems such as mass exploitation, decaying suburbs and the impoverishment of the Third World. The futility of teeny bopping, the swindling of ideology buddies – that's people's new drug of choice! I suppose that all that, today, makes you laugh somewhat. The sixties were wildly trendy. We glorify the nostalgia of that time now. A lack of concern? What lack of concern? And for whom? Thirty-five years on, I can't disagree with the adolescent that I was.

For me, Trans began to fade in my eighteenth year. I go to live abroad: Canada, Italy, Algeria. Five years of being far away from my family, except for some month-long stints at home in the summertime. One day, perhaps, I will talk about those years. Perhaps. But for now, my story is Trans and my family.

Far away from everyone, I live with my memories. I have thousands of images in my head, noises, and smells. I go over certain images, one road or another, one landscape or another, Mont-Saint-Michel in the mist, the pond at Villecartier, the castle at Combourg, the church square in Trans, the shops, the school, the farm where we went to get milk… My dreams are haunted by the small roads around Trans. I walk for hours and hours on these small roads between La Boussac, Pleine-Fougères and Vieux-Viel.

Moreover, there are the letters. We always wrote frequently to each other in our family, my mother, brothers and sisters. During the last years of boarding school, with Marie-Annick, Madeleine and Agnès, we'd send each other hilarious letters on fashion, all that was going on and the schemes of teenybopper friends. When we'd see each other, we'd continue the letters face to face. I found these letters some days ago, at the bottom of a drawer, in a cardboard box. I didn't know that I had kept them. I started opening envelops to read a few pages. But I quickly stopped. I couldn't go back to those years, to that happiness: too dangerous, too intense, too unbearable. All that wasn't said, behind those words. Everything that we did not to say to each other. Everything that we did not want to see. I put everything back into the box and closed the drawer. One day, perhaps….

One thing that happens when you are abroad and stay away from your family for months and months, is that letters become more personal, more intimate. As you don't see or don't speak to each other anymore, letters go straight to the point in this uninterrupted conversational space since childhood. Away from everyone, I have this feeling of a life which continues outside of me, which is mysterious. It is interwoven with rites and customs in which I no longer play a part. I feel that I am slowly detaching myself from a familiar everyday world, one that I will no longer recognise. So, these letters create another link and a new connection. My family write to me like someone who is no longer part of the clan, who is living something else, alone. And me? I suffer from both this separation and the realisation – albeit still somewhat unclear – of living for myself and confronting my freedom.

It is pure happiness to get back to Trans, to the house and everybody whenever I go back in the summer. To bathe in our old customs, enjoy our meals in the kitchen, our discussions, our laughs and our walks in the forest. Just like before. However, not totally: I feel like I'm just passing through. I know that I'm going to leave again and I feel slightly at odds. And then our family itself changes. We are no longer the same: over the years all of them get married or leave. That's how it goes, that's life. That's what happens in families. This changing time, like twilight, when one story is ending and another is just beginning. Our family is going to have to change. Agree to share memories and nostalgia whilst preparing for something else that you can hardly even imagine. And then Dad dies and my mother is alone.

And then there is Agnès. I understand, bit by bit, through letters, that she is not well, but not from a physical illness. Agnès has a sickness of the soul and of the mind. She doesn't know what she wants anymore or what she is living through. She slides little by little towards an absence of herself and of life. One day, I learn that she has been committed to a psychiatric clinic. Then she comes out. Then she goes back in. She alternates between phases of elation and then despair. She slowly moves into the abyss. From afar, I try to understand and take it in.

For me Agnès, had always been a girl who laughed, who joked and who was full of ideas. She had loads of friends, she was dynamic, and she wanted to make things and people move. We were so close, the two of us. We were such a pair. We had unending, rousing discussions. We had the same likes and dislikes. But maybe (I tell myself today) her joyfulness was forced. Maybe her laugh sounded false. Maybe she was, amongst us all, the one who had to pay the price with this schizophrenia in us: between our happiness of being together in Trans, and this black hole of unhappiness, this silence which gnawed on the inside, the hell at home. Maybe Agnès paid for all of us.

Going back to France one summer, I go to see her in the clinic. However, I don't recognise her. She seems so alone, so distressed, so totally terrified. She has this look which consumes her face, this call of her eyes as if to say, 'Do something, help me, I'm begging you. I don't know where I'm going or what I'm sinking into.' I want to take her out of this clinic, to save her and protect her. I can't tolerate this look. But to do what? Take her where? My mother, brothers and sisters are just as overwhelmed as I am, but they live with this suffering on a daily basis, month after month, not like me, from afar. Through letters. I feel like a coward, a simple pen pusher.

Sometimes, she improves and goes back to her former and normal life. She works, she travels. She laughs, she gets carried away and gets excited. And then she dissolves. Back to the clinic and the medication. Back to the fear and torment. And our family who feels utterly, utterly responsible.

Chapter 11

After five years, I come back to France for good. I settle in Paris, a place where I'd previously never set foot. For me, it was a little like a no man's land: I am back in France, but I am far from Brittany and family. I have no idea what to do with my life. But I need this space to find myself – I'll see later on. The first friends I make in Paris are all from the respectable left-bank middle class. It is just after May '68 (which I had spent in Algeria).

In May '68, my friends came out. It was their epic. They fought, they dreamed, they believed in the revolution. I have a great time with them. We are full of ideas and no doubt, we are going to achieve many things. Except that we are not from the same background. We are not from the same world. Everything seems easy to them, that is clear. They have this easy way with them which I have never seen before, unless in movies. They have big, beautiful apartments and are connected through all kinds of networks. They're on the right side. I'm in the middle of them, me. I feel like a neanderthal. We are a light year's distance from each other, socially and culturally. I don't think that they even think about it or realise it. They don't see that everything that is normal and natural to them is the complete opposite to me. It's like being at the zoo. It is a world away from receiving an award in the main courtyard at the Cordeliers School, in Dinan, with my mother in the middle of all those well-dressed people. It's practically another planet. I have to pinch myself every day, to realise that I am not in a film or a book. This world really exists. I have the feeling, amongst them, that I am studying ethnology. At the same time, they are my friends. And I will embark on a great adventure with them.

In June, after my exams, I go home to Brittany. After this immersion into middle class elixir, I have a need for ditches and sunken lanes, little lost roads, grocery stores where you can sit in and enjoy a chat, and wheat farms. I want to hear patois, see Gitanes cigarettes protruding from moustaches and see normal people again. And then, I am going to see my mother and family at the house again in Trans. I go back with Bernard, who is completing a work placement in Paris and one of his friends. We get into the friend's Renault 4 and go through the tunnel in Saint-Cloud. It is the beginning of summer, roll on Brittany. We don't get very far however. Coming out of Mortagne, on the way to Alençon, a bad bend in the road followed by a bad turn of the wheel and there you have it: the Renault 4 upside down in the ditch and me passed out. I wake up in the hospital in Mortagne. They ask me where I am sore and I respond by telling them that I am sore everywhere, which doesn't help the emergency surgeon very much. Thankfully, given the state I'm in, they see something that has to be done, they have to sew up my scalp. My head is seriously damaged with my scalp completely torn away from my skull. I am bleeding everywhere, and it hurts like hell. They bandage me up cartoon-style, leaving only my eyes free. They put me to bed with loads of pillows under my back to make it comfortable for my head. And then they say good night. Me? I think I'm going to die. Really. My back is so sore, that I can't breathe. I am certain that I am going to stay there. It's my brother (who walks away with a fractured shoulder) who calls for the doctor. They do an x-ray straight away which shows a fracture of the spinal column, which goes to show that they should have listened to me in the first place, when I said that I was sore all over. I'm fortunate however: the spinal cord is untouched. All there is to do is wait until it mends itself. It will take some time.

So there you have it: I spend a good part of summer '69 in hospital and then in a clinic. I am full of medication to relieve the pain and help me to get some sleep. I cannot move a muscle, not even my arms. My mother and Agnès come to see Bernard and me at the hospital in Mortagne. They ask me to tell them what happened. I haven't the slightest as I have partial amnesia. I haven't the vaguest memory of leaving Paris nor of the accident. A few hours of my life are wiped out forever, but I don't complain. I just find it a little strange. A blackout.

I am alone at the clinic in Mans. I am in a million pieces, but I feel safe. I float in a strange world, an interim of sorts. It's summer and very hot, but they take good care of me. I am living in the moment and not thinking of the future. I am there, that's all. When I start getting a little bit better, I read the poems of Emily Dickinson at night before dark. I start relearning how to move. They make me sit up in bed, then onto the side of the bed. They make me stand up. Then one step, then another in the corridor. Then the stairs. I am afraid, I think I am going to hurt myself. But my body holds up.

In this clinic in the summer of '69, I feel like I'm in a dream. With my head fried, my back in a brace, the heat, distant noises from outside, the poems of Emily Dickinson, I float along as if I am weightless. This image comes back to me at times, this flash in my head: in the ambulance, just after the accident, during a brief moment of consciousness, I say to myself: I'll soon know. Yes, I say to myself, I will soon know what lies ahead.

When I get out of the clinic, I go to Trans. It's not really the return I had dreamed of during my five years away. I am so sore that I don't see or hear anything. Having departed the reassuring bubble of the clinic, I am cold. I shiver and endure nightmares. I don't want to talk or explain. I go round in circles and bump into walls. Outside, I sleepwalk. I feel so far from trees, fields, ditches. I get the feeling that I am no longer capable of touching things. Never have I felt this feeling of distance, as if I were a stranger here in Trans with my family. My body needs to reaccustom itself. I have to relearn happiness and I don't know if I will make it or how long it will take me. I don't live in my body anymore. I am nowhere. I am no-one. I no longer even have the wonder of memories. If only I could sleep. But I come out sweaty on cold nights where all I do is chase phantoms. Tell me, will all this ever come to an end?

Chapter 12

B
ut of course, you recover – blindly, gropingly, knocking into things, relapsing. Yes, you recover eventually. You emerge from the nightmare piece by piece. You don't know how you did or how it happened. But one day, you understand that it's over – even though nothing, of course, is ever over. Suddenly you have a thousand urges, a thousand desires. You get high on projects. You get caught up with a whirlwind of encounters. You say that anything is possible once more. My opportunity came in Paris at the beginning of the seventies – this bubbling excitement post-1968. Everyone is moving. Everyone is bursting at the seams. We have everything to do and everything to imagine. I immerse myself in politics, cinema, music, writing. Life is electric, compulsive. Leftist militantism, living in communities, zen Buddhism, wholegrain rice, hippies, anti-fascist rallies, poetry, cinema reviews…Paris is in party mode.

Trans seems so far away to me, but I go back there from time to time. At Christmas for example, when all the family gathers around my mother. But I feel like I'm moving away. That my life is elsewhere. Country-bumpkin in Paris, a Parisian in Brittany: curious role-plays, of which I try to pick out the best one. A part of me feels like a traitor. I develop reflexes, a way of talking, a way of seeing things from another world. I have old country desires some evenings and certain memories which break my heart: to have time, to run away from the glitz, the nonsense, the trappings of fashion. But there is fear at the same time, of uncovering too many ghosts, of being drawn to too many old stories or to stories that are buried too deeply. In Paris, I create a new life. Even if I feel, at times, as though I am in transit. Not from here, not from there. And yet it suits me.

However, there is one thing which I cannot get used to: seeing my friends' fathers, to see, sometimes, one or other of my friends with their father. I watch them. I listen to them talking to each other, and I imagine the bond they enjoy. They are young, both of them. I watch them. I listen to them. I think of all these years that they have spent together, and to all those that await them. I would like to know what that is like. What it is that like to have your father when you are twenty years old or twenty-five years old. Rather than hurt me, I find it altogether more of a surprise. I watch them as though they are acting in a movie. Like they are not father and son for real. I find it strange to see them together. I am living a real life – there can't be another one. Alone, without my father.

In the Spring of '72, while on holiday in the Massif Central, I spend a night with some friends in Aurillac. In fact, because of an intense appendicitis, I am forced to stay for a fortnight, after a week in hospital. It is there, at my friend's house, that I receive a letter from my mother, posted from Trans on April 15th. She jokes about my forced stay in Aurillac, which she labels my 'last escapade'. Then she adds (I also kept this letter). 'I too have a kind of escapade myself: I must undergo a medical procedure at the clinic in Combourg, due to an ulcer in my stomach. I hope I'll get through it…..But I probably won't be back in Trans for a fortnight. Well, I'll finish here, I must let the family know what's happening. I'll not be short of visits at the clinic anyhow. It will not affect me one way or the other!'

I didn't know that she was sick. It's true that my mother is not the type to complain. It's also true, that I don't see her as much now. As soon as I get better, I'll go see her. Some days later, I get a letter from my brother Jacques. 'Mum must have written to you last week that she was going into the clinic at the start of this week to get her stomach ulcer operated on. She was supposed to get the operation yesterday. Bernard called me there a while ago: the surgeons did not remove the ulcer as they realised, on the operation table, that she has widespread cancer. Operating is out of the question. According to them, there is nothing they can do. They are giving her two months max.'

I read the letter over and over. I keep having trouble with the words: 'widespread cancer', 'two months maximum'. How can I believe it? How can I accept it? My mother can't die, she hasn't the right to die.

She is hardly sixty years old; she is strong, she takes care of us all, she is the liveliest out of all of us. She has a right to live and a right to happiness more than any of us. Things like this can't happen: a little operation and dead in two months. Impossible. Doctors say anything and they have no right to. I want to be with my brothers and sisters right now, to feel among them and stop the doctors from saying whatever it is that they are saying. Moreover, Jacques tells me, the surgeons took the responsibility of hiding the truth from my mother. They told her that they had removed the ulcer and that the operation had gone well. They are presenting us with a done deal; condemned to lie, just like them.

I read and then reread these two letters, that of my mother and that of Jacques. I would love to leave straight away and not lose a single second of this time which now is so precious. I need to go to Trans quickly. I need to go back to the house, to my mother and to everyone. But I cannot move. In any case, there is no-one there in Trans. My mother, upon her departure from the clinic, goes to Saint-Brieuc, to Jean and Denise's house, for what she believes to be her convalescence. In Trans, the house is empty. And my mother is going to die.

Then finally, I am able to leave. I hurry to Saint-Brieuc. I embrace my mother, I look at her and listen to her. She laughs and jokes and recounts her 'escapade' – the operation of this ulcer which they removed. She says that she is making the most out of this period of détente at Jean and Denise's, where they are taking great care of her and where she doesn't have to do any cooking or housework. Naturally, once she's well rested, she will go back to Trans and all will be like before – a tranquil life – where, I swear, I will go more often. I watch her and listen to her, but I don't know if I will be able to lie. Mum? She doesn't lie, she actually thinks that everything is going to start up again just like before. However, over these next few months which – according to the doctors – we have left with her, we are going to have to lie. Is it even imaginable, to not talk openly to each other, to not speak the truth when death is so close at hand? All the while, she is laughing and joking. She doesn't seem like someone who is about to die. What if the doctors are wrong?

What if they are saying all kinds of nonsense? I don't want to believe them. After all, doctors make mistakes sometimes; it does happen. After all, my mother was seriously ill in Teilleul and she got better. So, why not this time? Why can there not be another miracle? I nearly start to believe it. But I'll believe it when I see it.

On Mother's Day, we decide to have a great family reunion in Saint-Brieuc. Since my father's passing, we have continued to get together in Trans for Christmas. I can't remember under which pretext we found to convince her that this year, it would be best for all of us to assemble in Saint-Brieuc for Mother's Day. For us, of course, it is the urgency of it all. My mother will no longer be with us, no doubt at Christmas. I start to really believe the doctors: my mother is often tired and disheartened. She no longer has her get-up-and-go or her good humour. She is suffering. She is worried. Everyone will be at this party. Even Marie-Annick, who has been living in Wales since she got married. We had to find another pretext to justify her presence at a simple Mother's Day gathering. Marie-Annick knows that it will probably be the last time she will see her, but my mother doesn't know. Everyone will be there. And to begin with, I have to introduce Anne to my mother. I have often spoken to her about Anne, but she still hasn't met her. We are supposed to be getting married in a few months. For Anne, it's vital that she sees her – and heart-breaking.

I don't remember much of the party itself except for this combination of happiness and fatigue in my mother and a forced and desperate gaiety in us. You can now see the illness in her face and in her gestures. We all want to cry. But instead we laugh, we joke and we talk too loudly. My mother is with us. Even so, she is a little absent in her look. Is she starting to doubt something? I haven't a clue. I look at her. I don't want to think about the days ahead, the days that remain.

In July, I shoot a film with Yves, my old friend from boarding school in Brittany. And a third guy, who in our eyes, has the advantage of having a camera. A film cobbled together with no money. With absolutely nothing at all. A film of which the spools sleep in an attic today, somewhere in Brittany. On our journey from Paris, we stop by Trans to spend the night. The house is empty. It is the first time, in all my life, to sleep in our house when it is empty. I never had that feeling up until now. Before, coming home to Trans always meant getting back to the family. At least to get back to my mother. But his time the house is empty. It feels deserted and soulless to me. I want to flee, as quickly and as far away as possible. I understand that it's the end; that the house will no longer be ours – that of childhood, happiness, and unhappiness. It's over. I already feel like a stranger. Quick, let's get out of here. This house smells of death.

We shoot our cobbled film fifty kilometres south of Saint-Brieuc. I go up to Jean and Denise's regularly to see my mother. She is suffering more and more now. She is asking what's going on. She is eager to get back to Trans, to get back to her little ways and settle back into her life. But she senses quite adroitly that something's not right. I wonder if she is taken in by what the doctors have told her and that which we play on her. Never, however, do I dare speak to her about it honestly. We keep up the pretence, through anxiety and fear. She is now almost always in bed. She has no more energy to joke. She says that it is taking some time to recuperate after having had such a simple procedure. And then she looks at me: I need to reassure her, her eyes say. She is begging me to reassure her. Or does she want me to tell her the truth? I leave the house full of rage and shame. I don't want my mother to die.

One Saturday, on set, I feel consumed with panic; a panic which takes me by the throat, a premonition. I have to leave straight away with a steady walk. All throughout the journey to Saint-Brieuc, my heart races. Quick, quick, quicker. I go into her bedroom. My mother is alive. She is in bed, in pain. She tells me she is in pain and that she doesn't understand why. My uncle is there by her side. My father's brother who is a priest. He imparts words of consolation to her, or what he thinks are words of consolation. He talks to her about God and about Jesus on the cross. My mother looks at him steely. I have never seen this look before. She tells him that he can keep his words for himself, that she doesn't see what God has to do in all this, that religion, in any case…..I have never heard my mother speak like this or use words like these before. These few words that she utters to my uncle in a low tone, and this look that's so rigid. It's like I'm seeing someone else and not my mother. The suffering and death which prowls, which she feels prowling around, plunges her into this great silence – this great silence which I read in her eyes. My uncle, disconcerted, mumbles some words mechanically and departs. I stay with her, not knowing what to say, except for some gauche words from a son to his mother, who wants to tell her how much he loves her but who doesn't know how to. We're well versed in words in our family, but have we ever really spoken to each other? I go back onto the set in the evening reassured – I really thought I was going to find her dead – and frozen at the same time with anxiety: what was this premonition which made me rush and drive like a madman?

The next day, right at the beginning of the afternoon, I see Madeleine coming. We have to go immediately to Saint-Brieuc as mother is dying. I hear this sentence in my head (she's dying) all along the fifty kilometres. I think of nothing else. I don't want to think of anything else. However, I get there too late. My mother has just passed. Her last words, Jean tells me, were for Agnès, who was beside her. Agnès who battles with her own pain, this shadow which engulfs her. I look at my mother. I think back to our conversation from yesterday, to these measly few words that we exchanged. I would have cursed myself for the rest of my life if I hadn't have come, if I hadn't have had this final conversation with her. She has just died, however I think in my despair she might still be living and so incredulously I lie in wait for a sign, a quiver, a breath of life. But no, it's over. My mother is dead. She is sixty years old. My father has been dead for exactly ten years. I am twenty-five years old and I no longer have my parents. All of that goes round my head; dates and numbers. I will never see her again. My mother is dead. It's over. My mother will not live, she will not enjoy life again. Her life, that of the sun, the flowers, the garden, the neighbours, summer outdoor conversations, the meals, the crazy laughs, the chicken yard, the chitchat in the shops, everyone's life journey, the holidays, the wooden floor in the kitchen, the polishing of the shrapnel, the flowers on the table. Life. I go out of the house; I walk straight ahead and cry. My mother didn't have the right to die. She loved life too much. She had years of happiness ahead of her in Trans. My mother is dead and I can't accept it. I have nothing more to say.

We all get together, us brothers and sisters. We have to keep warm. We have to prepare for the burial. And then for the great emptiness thereafter. What is a family without parents? What keeps a family together? There will be no more annual gatherings for us or visits to Trans. There will be no more holidays to Trans. Parents are the history of the family. This is our history. Since my father died, my mother played the role on her own: she was our beacon, the fulcrum, who enabled everything to make sense. We know that she is in Trans, that she is waiting for us and that we will go and see her. We will gather round her. We will laugh, we will joke, we will walk with her in the forest and at the pond at Villecartier. We will go into the yard and feed the hens and the rabbits. We will watch her prepare the soup in the evening, while discussing the little things which happened in the day, the trivial endeavours of life. But my mother is dead. And we are alone.

Here we all are for the burial in Trans – ten years after the death of my father. We gather at the house, but each room, each piece of furniture, each object is a farewell. This house is no longer ours. My mother's shadow is everywhere, her voice and her silence. Without her, this house is dead. We embrace each other in the house. We talk and make noise, but we know that we will be chased out of there like out of paradise lost.

The church is full, as it was for my father. All these people from Trans and local villages. I have lost track of them a little and no longer know them all that well. I have the feeling of re-discovering myself in seeing them again, of renewing my life in Trans; all these country peoples' faces, artisans, friends from school who have grown up and become men. And at the same time, I know that this mass is a farewell to Trans, that the line has been drawn and I will only be a passer-by from now on. This church where I made my debut as a choirboy, where I served at mass, at vespers and complines so many times but I already feel like a stranger. And this weight of the burial service, this ghastly death ritual, so solemn and so morbid. This chilling yoke suddenly on your shoulders – such a glacial chill throughout your body. I feel this crowd of men and women in black behind me who have come to say good-bye to my mother, and it is a presence which warms, which comforts, but I know deep down that it is also a farewell to our family, our family who was, for some years from Trans.

In the little cemetery on the way out of town, my mother is buried alongside my father in the same grave. There they are both reunited in death – they who so loved each other and afterwards so hated each other. I don't know what memories of my father my mother held on to over the years. I never spoke to her about him. I could never talk about the war between them. It was like a great big stone block – impossible to shift. You hope that little by little, the block would move itself. But the years go by. And then it is too late.

In this little cemetery where, light years ago I used to nick the little cherubs off childrens' graves, they are both interred now side by side, my mother and father. And our childhood too, interred with them.

One day we start the grieving process at the house and go from room to room, one last time; open wardrobes, cupboards, pull out drawers one last time. Close our eyes and dream about what life was like here all together; the laughs, the meals, the friends, coming back for holidays, nights spent reading and talking. And then the cries. The blow-ups in the evening when my father came home. Go up to the attic, one last time, where we played so much, in the middle of the harnesses, the collars of draught horses, magical and mysterious games which was like our other hidden life. One last farewell to my windowless room, where I was during the holidays, encapsulated in a bubble of happiness. And then go out by the back door, go across the Pleine-Fougères road, push open the small door to enter into the yard. And get hit suddenly with all these memories of communal games. Be welcomed by laughs and little childish chats that we used to have back then, in amongst the hens and the caged rabbits. To say farewell, still, even if it's impossible, because we do not say farewell to our childhood. We live with it each day of our lives.

The house, it's over: we have decided to sell it. A decision taken like in other families, when the parents have died. There you go, we're selling up. Everyone takes what they want, in equal share – a wardrobe, a bed, a table. I don't take anything. I don't want anything. The house in Trans? I have it entirely in my head. But I don't want other people to buy it, live there, reside there, fill it with their dreams, their games, their habits. I could not tolerate that. In fact, if I took anything from the house in Trans it is the following: the big photo of my parent's wedding, in its original frame. I have it in front of me on my desk. But I have a lot of trouble looking at it. They are so young, so beautiful and so fragile with their half-smile to the photographer and to their future life together. The frame is wonky and the photo is stained and torn in parts. I don't want to touch or restore it. It is the photo of broken happiness. It is the photo of my parents.

Chapter 13

There you have it; it's done. One day, I learn that the house has been sold. I don't know who bought it, who has moved in, who is now making memories there and I don't want to know. Sometimes whenever I go back to Brittany, to see my brothers and sisters, I happen to pass by Trans. However, I cannot stop by the front of the house, I cannot look at it. When I look back I can see us sitting on the footpath on a Sunday evening, reading our books or magazines, whilst my mother talks to Madam Boucher from the other side of the street. Madam Boucher is a haberdasher; she sells buttons, string, stockings, handkerchiefs. Her husband is a shoemaker and when you go into his workshop, you are hit by the smell of leather and adhesive, mixed in with his Gitane Maïs cigarette. In Madam Boucher's home there is a depository of books – a little country library. Books and comics are arranged on two shelves amongst boxes of spools of thread and buttons. To get your hands on a few books, you only have to cross the street. We are always hanging around Madam Boucher's. It is this image which follows me whenever I cross the street in Trans, without looking at the house where strangers now live. Usurpers. The joy of reading in the evening on the footpath and the conversational flow between my mother and Madam Boucher. It's like a stab in the back which goes completely through me. I cannot stop before the house; I have to get out of there fast.

At night in Paris, I often dream about the little roads around Trans that we used to wander through, us children, crisscrossing our magical kingdom. It is like a labyrinth in my dreams. I walk tirelessly, I get lost, I go round in circles, I hesitate at each crossroads, I take a wrong turn. I have lost my way. I dream about my mother as well, of course. She is living in Trans. I go back on holiday, I push open the door and she is waiting for me, sitting at the kitchen table, sewing and darning. But at the same time, I know that it isn't real, that she is not there. Everything erupts into fear and anxiety. My mother is a ghost, no words come out of her mouth. I cry in silence.

I married Anne a few months after my mother's passing and no-one or anything can make amends for this injustice: that of my mother's absence at our wedding. I have to get used to no longer having parents. I have to forget that I could have come home with Anne. I need to forget what they could have said to each other, Anne and my mother, in secret. I have to forget my life in Trans.

In any case, I am becoming Parisian. I still need to have little jaunts to Brittany, to my brother's and sister's houses, but it is no longer my home. Paris is home for me, where I continue however – for several years – to not just feel myself, a little off-kilter. In Brittany, I almost never talk about my life in Paris. It is such a different world, another story. I like coming back to Brittany to see the trees, the ditches, the light, the people in the market in Dol, their words and gestures. But my life is in Paris – the helter-skelter of life.

My brothers and sisters rarely come to Paris. The person who comes most often is Agnès. She comes to me for help because she feels lost. Since my mother's passing, she alternates stays in psychiatric clinics with attempts at 'normal' life. She plunges into complete despair and then experiences periods of unbridled exhilaration. A few years ago, she was able to work, even if it was with difficulty. Today, however, it's impossible. She is constantly on edge, on the brink of the abyss. She tries to figure out what to do with her life, between a thirst for perfection and true meaning, and a fear of failure. She stays in a religious community for a time then becomes embroiled with a sect but gets out at the last moment. She is lost within herself and within the world. She demands too much of herself and too much of the world. Agnès; so funny, so passionate, so generous when we were children and then adolescents. Agnès, for whom I can no longer find the words, who I see escaping, drowning, without being able to do anything. She has to be saved, but I don't know how. I don't know if it's even possible. In Brittany, my brothers and sisters do their best but they despair. When she comes to Paris, I feel reprehensibly powerless.

One evening, at the end of one of her visits with us, Anne, upon returning home from work, finds her unconscious, lying down in the kitchen, close to the gas oven which is still hissing. When I get home, the firemen are there. They tell me that she is alive and that they are taking her to hospital. They hold out a letter that she had written to me that she had left on the table and it says that she does not want to return to the clinic. That she would prefer to die. I get into the ambulance with her, but I am unable to think of anything. I am in the ambulance with Agnès and that's all I know. I am beside her when she regains consciousness in the hospital, after having been taken out of danger. I look at her. She looks at me, but I can't get a single word out. The only one which presses on my lips and bangs about in my head is: why? But I can't say it. Maybe it's because I don't want to hear the answer. We look at each other in this hospital ward. She is coming back from death. But how do I welcome her back to life when I can see in her eyes that she is close to death? We look at each other for a long time, for an eternity. All of our life passes by in this exchange of looks; our childhood, our games, our laughs, everything that we have done together. Our dreams – ah, our dreams! All that we would do when we would get older. Agnès, don't go. Stay with us. Please.

We find a new clinic, near Paris, to give her time to recuperate and get back on her feet. It is a beautiful clinic, surrounded by a big garden. But the clinics are always beautiful and the gardens are always big. That's what I read in Agnès' gaze, whenever I say goodbye to her, whenever she gives me a little sign with her hand as if to say: What am I going to do here in this beautiful clinic, in this big garden? What is it going to change for me? I found a letter which she had sent me the previous year, from another clinic. She wrote: 'If you have a brainy idea to get me out of this bloody mess…. for where I am now is not pretty.' No, I have no idea. How I feel like a right bastard, leaving her here in this clinic. But I don't know what else I can do. Is there anything else that can be done? Can someone tell me?

One day Agnès leaves the clinic and goes back to Brittany. She tries to live, at last. Then she goes into another clinic, where she has already spent days, weeks and months. She gets out, comes to Paris, then returns to the clinic with its big garden.

One evening in March '79, I get a telephone call from Madeleine: the clinic has just warned her that Agnès has not returned since last evening. She went for a walk as normal but she should have come back late afternoon. She hasn't been seen since. The clinic notified the police and fire brigade but they don't find her. Nothing. No trace. No clue. I tell myself that perhaps she took the train to Paris. That perhaps she is in Montparnasse sick or lost. I take my car and head straight for Montparnasse. I search the station from top to bottom. I wait for arriving trains, on the platform, I go back ten or twenty times to the waiting room and to the bar buffet. What I do makes no sense whatsoever, I know full well, but how can I wait and do nothing?

The next morning, I take the first train for Rennes. It is an interminable trip, all this lost time when this is urgent. And, at the same time, a grace period before the inevitable, I can feel it. In Rennes, I meet up with Jean and Bernard. We go to the clinic straightaway, where they tell us that nothing more can be done, that all the searches have been halted, that she will not be found. So, we decide ourselves to go look for her, cursing these good-for-nothings who throw in the towel and resign themselves. A river crosses the big garden at the clinic, then continues through woodland and fields. Without thinking too much, and because we have to to start somewhere, we follow the river. Beyond the garden, barely one hundred metres away we pass by a bridge. Instinctively, we look at the water, below. There, in the middle of some branches held back by grass, a spot of colour appears. Our hearts are in our mouths: it is Agnès' coat. We look more closely, maybe it's a simple piece of cloth, a piece of fabric fallen into the river. We lean over and look. We think we are going to die: yes, it's Agnès' coat. It's Agnès, held back by the branches in the middle of the river. We can't move or speak. One of us begins, in a low voice, 'It looks like Agnès.' Someone replies: 'You think it is her?' followed by: 'Yes, it's her.' We remain on the bridge, hypnotised, petrified. But we have to move, do something, alert someone. We cross the bridge. Upstream, on the edge of the water at a little inlet, we suddenly spot an open umbrella, set on the sand. It's Agnès'. She came this far in the rain, put down her umbrella onto the sand and entered the water. She let herself be taken. I cry, seeing this umbrella. I want to scream. I can't imagine Agnès entering the water and being taken away.

The few seconds that we remain there, frozen, at the river's edge, seems like an eternity to us. Then, in one fell swoop, in one movement, we leave and run towards the clinic. We move as though in a dream or a nightmare. It can't be us here on this riverside. It can't be Agnès in the middle of this river. When we alert the director of the clinic – who doesn't seem to believe us – it is as though someone else is in speaking to her. So, we call the emergency services ourselves, who, in turn don't believe us either. They scoured the place in their search for Agnès and found nothing. We must be mistaken, after all it's only a piece of cloth. We need to calm ourselves and trust them. But the nightmare endures: why do we have to be there on the phone, trying to convince the emergency services that it is really our sister who we've just seen drowned in the river? Why are we compelled to provide details to justify ourselves, when all we wish is to leave, vomit and hide somewhere?

Finally, they allow themselves to be convinced and we gather on the bridge, looking like we did before at the spot of colour in the middle of the branches. They take a long pole and attempt to reach and grab the cloth. They move the branches apart and all of a sudden Agnès' body appears. This time it is certain. It is undoubtedly her, squeezed into her coat. However, they go about it the wrong way, and Agnès, freed from the branches, is taken by the current and gently goes under the bridge with the flow of the water, colliding with the grass and the reeds. Drowned Agnès escaping, disappearing – a splash of colour carried by the river. The firemen run along the riverbank. People are there – who watch, point, comment, chat and call out to one another. I want to shout out, 'Get away from here. Clear off. It's my sister who has died. It's my sister who has killed herself. Leave. You have nothing to do here. Let me be. Leave us with her.'

Finally, at the next bridge, the firemen manage to stop her. They grasp her and pull her up. And there she is, lifeless at their feet – at our feet. Agnès who has died and whom I cannot look at. I cannot look at her face, it's impossible. I can't do it and I don't want to. Here the three of us are, Jean, Bernard and me, incapable of looking at her and incapable of looking at ourselves. Thankfully, after that everything flies by. With professional technical moves, Agnès' body is carried by the firemen to the ambulance. Everything goes so fast. We must get out of there. We must forget all the onlookers who watch and wait. We must get out now.

Then there is the autopsy, along with the list of medicine consumed. There are policemen, paperwork, a process. And so we find ourselves all together once more, amongst brothers and sisters due to a death in the family. We need to think of the funeral. We need to plan the funeral. Does the church even authorise masses for the burial of a suicide? The rector in Trans, who knew me as an altar boy, who knows us all and who knew Agnès, does not worry about the church's doctrine. And we gather, once more, in the church in Trans for a burial. But this time, it's one of us, the children, who has died. It is Agnès, the most fragile of all of us. Who suffered more than any of us. Who so loved life and happiness. And for whom, life and happiness were denied. Agnès, to whom my mother reached out just before she died. Why her? Why was this mound of unhappiness placed on her head? Why did we not know how to protect her from unhappiness? What should we have done?

She is buried in the little cemetery in Trans, beside our parents, where there is both too much love and too little love amongst these three adjoining graves. There are now, these three names inscribed on three headstones in the cemetery in Trans: Henri Rémond, Angèle Rémond, Agnès Rémond. I hardly ever go there. I don't like depositing flowers onto graves, standing in front of graves, and looking at these three names on the graves. I curse death. I curse graves.

Chapter 14

I have these photos, that I look at furtively – that I can only look at furtively. These photos of happiness in Trans, in the kitchen or in front of the house, a day in blissful sunshine or at the edge of the lake at Villecartier in the forest. Us children, bound together by our history, from Mortain and the adventure of the war and the landing, to the paradise of games, of dreams, of rites and secrets. My mother in the sun, petting the dog. And then this photo of my father, not long before his passing in a black suit, a little to the side of the family. He is smiling, or at least he is trying to smile. You can already see the shadow of death on his face, but he is smiling bravely; my father who I didn't know how to love. I have been dreaming of him a lot recently. In my dreams, he is at the house in Trans, waiting for me. He is waiting for something from me. He is the same age as he was when he died, the age I am today. We are therefore the same age: fifty-three years old and we are alone. I am unnerved to know that he is there as I don't know what to say to him. I am afraid that the scenes I witnessed as a child will brew up again, whenever he used to fight with my mother. But he waits, he relies on me, he is trusting. I wonder what I must do for him? What must I do for my father?

I wrote this book to finish with the war. The house in Mortain has been destroyed, the house in Teilleul has been destroyed and the house in Trans has been sold. My father is dead, my mother is dead and my sister is dead. I want to live in peace with everyone, the living and the dead.

About the author

A devoted Francophile, Anne-Marie Faulkner achieved her dream of becoming a fluent French speaker by living in Paris. During her Master's in Translation at Queen's Belfast, an original copy of Alain Rémond's *Chaque Jour est un Adieu* re-surfaced, triggering her unequivocal admiration for the story. Identifying parallels between the author's upbringing in Brittany and her own in Co Donegal, she set out to translate and then publish the very first copy of *Each Day is a Farewell* into English. She lives in Moville.